DEATH THROWS NO SHADOW

Once again Mike Capper, the Fleet Street free-lance who has appeared in several Leo Grex thrillers, returns to provide a focus for action. This time he is after Baroness Rorthy's incredible personal story. However, after making a surprise rendezvous with her following a phone call for help, he finds himself confronted by the notorious Andy Beecham, whose Casino Palace is London's latest fashionable fun-spot for those with cash or credit to lose.

Another woman arrives hurriedly—Stella Daly, who once in the past almost became Mrs Capper. It is Stella who is responsible for bringing Chief Superintendent Gary Bull and his assistant Inspector Bert Whitelaw into a thriller where mystery is attended by menace and murder. There is some expert double dealing by villains whose known operations are only surface play to conceal a scheme that is intended to make use of North Sea oil for a purpose not included in the oil men's plans.

A story packed with drama and baffling incident that moves at a cracking pace towards a surprising conclusion.

DEATH THROWS
NO SHADOW

by

LEO GREX

ROBERT HALE . LONDON

© Leo Grex 1976
First published in Great Britain 1976

ISBN 0 7091 5875 0

Robert Hale Limited
Clerkenwell House
Clerkenwell Green
London EC1R 0HT

Printed in Great Britain by Northumberland Press Ltd, Gateshead
and bound by Richard Clay (The Chaucer Press) Ltd, Bungay,
Suffolk

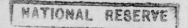

CHAPTER ONE

Mike Capper was engrossed in one of his favourite pastimes. He was staring through his uncurtained window down into the choked canyon of Fleet Street. The polluted atmosphere of the Street of Ink was more than usually thick with petrol smog. It was thick enough to taste. Almost to chew.

The ringing of his phone brought Capper's gaze away from the window just when he had decided he had better make the effort and shut it.

He reached out and lifted the receiver, and a voice he recognized said, 'Mike?' with a predictable touch of impatience. He not only recognized the voice, but also the tone. Tom Valence, the news editor of the *Daily Signet*, was not only short of patience, but also breath. That meant he had been having an argument, probably upstairs with the Big Man himself, who was the publisher of both the *Daily* and *Sunday Signet* as well as a string of magazines ranging from trade papers to glossy journals for females who liked to think of themselves as sophisticated.

'You struck dumb?' Valence snorted.

'Not quite. But the damned smog outside is doing its best. You're lucky to have an air-conditioned—'

'Crap! Cut it and do me a service,' the *Signet*'s news editor growled. 'Just tell me where you've got with the Rorthy wench. You promised to contact me and I don't like having to remind any writer who's grabbed a commission from me that he's expected to produce. Agree?'

Something must have really crawled under Valence's thick skin and dug in.

'I've made contact, Tom. I've set up a meet for tomorrow, and she sounded sympathetic to the idea when I last spoke to her.'

'Well, that's progress of sorts I suppose. If she gives you the story we'll have to get it vetted by our tame legal eagle. Make sure she understands the score. And, Mike, handle the gambling angle like a freshly wakened rattlesnake. You know Laughing Boy's reputation.' Tom Valence cleared his throat. 'Be hearing from you. 'Bye.'

The phone against Capper's ear clicked and he hung up.

Laughing Boy was Valence's cynical name for Andy Beecham, who had been buying up casino interests in Britain and collecting a great deal of publicity in the process. Particularly when he hired the lovely Baroness Rorthy as a scintillating croupier for his Casino Palace in Mayfair. The Baroness was almost unbelievably photogenic and in the past had provided great copy for the media.

She was an English girl from Midhurst in Sussex who had married the English-born Hungarian racing driver, Baron Rorthy, who had succeeded to a medieval title on the death of his parents in a plane crash in the United States. After thirty-five days of married life with the girl from Sussex the Baron had died when his Formula Three car overturned on a rain-wet circuit in Italy. The international school of photographers at the funeral had taken about six shots of the widow for every one of the flower-decked bier.

6

Then the Baroness, who had been variously reported as going into films, becoming a TV personality with her own programme, going round the world in a sailing craft, accepting an offer of marriage from a Greek shipping millionaire, and joining a world-renowned fashion house, an American PR firm, and a South American group of freedom fighters, had become a croupier for the man who was said to be crazy about her.

At that stage Tom Valence decided her exclusive story with pictures could do something to increase the *Daily Signet*'s circulation in an age of rising paper prices and national inflation. He had offered Mike Capper the commission, to be handled as a freelance. Capper knew why. A staff man hunting such a series could waste weeks only to learn the lady had changed her mind. Or had it changed for her.

Anyway, he'd be better able to judge the risk in a few hours. He had an appointment with the Rorthy wench, as Valence usually referred to her, at ten-thirty the next morning. He had spent most of a week getting that far without letting the rest of the Fleet Street wolf pack sniff out what he was doing, and so far he hadn't met the lady in the flesh, as it's called. He hadn't even met her in her croupier's spangles and see-through gown or one of the trousered suits that had been featured in the dailies and on TV at the time she was reported as heading off in the direction of a pricey executive's job in *haute couture*. He had talked to her on a variety of phones, always with his fingers crossed, and only two days before had been getting steadily nowhere when she suddenly changed. Her deep contralto had almost become excited. She had wanted a number she could

7

call. She had also wanted to know how long it would take to prepare the proposed series.

Out of the blue she had called to ask if he was married, and when he hesitated rather diffidently said caustically, 'Well, are you or aren't you? Or can't you remember?'

He had felt like swearing at her and telling her he hadn't the slightest interest in writing her damned story. But then he had thought of the figure Tom Valence had mentioned, with a share in subsidiary rights, and had hung on to his temper.

'I can remember very well,' he had heard himself saying with a calm that shook him more violently than anger. 'I was all set to let my intended make an honest man of me when there was the offer of a series. I said no very firmly, that I was getting ready for a honeymoon on the Costa del Sol, and then the bombshell exploded. Because I had turned down the chance of doing the series the woman I had been about to marry seized it. She was a section editor on a woman's magazine. She made a first-class job of it too. But she still hasn't collected a husband, only the reputation of being a bitch who is never really in heat.'

When he stopped speaking to her she asked, 'Is that an answer to my question?' ·

'I think so.'

'Then I'll see you at ten-thirty in two days' time.'

'Where?'

'At my flat. You'd better write down the address.'

He had done so. In fact, he had written it down twice. Once in his office address book and once on a slip of paper which was now in his wallet.

'Oh, by the way,' she had said before hanging up.

'I'm not using my married name as a tenant. At home I'm Miss Baynard.'

Then she had hung up, leaving him to recall that the girl from Midhurst had been Elsie Baynard. Due to a poor phone connection a local journalist had spelled the first name as Elise, and the error had been compounded. The Baron Josef Rorthy had even married Elise Baynard. And according to newspapers and radio announcers in various tongues it had been Elise Baynard who had mourned him at the graveside in Italy. Capper didn't have to be told it was Miss Elise, and not Elsie, Baynard who was the tenant of the flat whose address was in his wallet.

Another strong whiff of Fleet Street smog assailed his nostrils and played havoc with the mucous membranes of his nose and throat. He was on the point of forcing himself to rise and slam the window shut when the phone rang again. He reached for the receiver mechanically.

'I'm out,' he said abruptly.

'So am I. That makes two of us,' said a low feminine voice that both charmed and intrigued his ear.

'Think of the devil!' he exclaimed.

'The devil's a male, Mr Capper. There's nothing male about me, I assure you.'

'Consider me corrected and trying to think of an apology you might deem suitable, Miss Baynard.'

'Don't waste any more time. Just get into a taxi and drive to the Burlington Gardens Arcade. I'll be there waiting for you.'

'Can you tell me what's happened?' asked Capper, who had previously suffered from females' notions of what they considered to be urgent.

'Not on the phone.'

'I've a car parked in Shoe Lane, at the back of here. I'll collect it and be with you in a quarter of an hour— if the traffic's kind.'

She beat him to the click. He sat for five seconds playing over on mental recall the sound of her voice. She had sounded like someone who could be in trouble. Or that was the impression he had received.

He took a key from his pocket, unlocked the bottom drawer of his desk, and from under a collection of grubby paperbacks and some spare reams of typing paper, used notebooks, old calendars, a plastic bag of clean handkerchiefs, and some cuttings he had not got around to filing in his somewhat primitive but very personal filing system, reached for a cold metal shape which he withdrew.

He checked the snub-nosed Smith and Wesson thirty-eight, thumbed the safety, and rolled the filled cylinder. On his way to the door he dropped the gun in his hip pocket. He was, so far as he knew, the only journalist in Fleet Street to take a gun on some of his assignments, but then maybe some of the others were as close-mouthed about life and death details as Mike Capper. He couldn't even begin to guess.

He picked up his two-year-old Capri Ghia from the end of the archway where it was parked by arrangement with a foreman on the *Daily Signet*'s warehouse staff, drove up into Holborn, and in New Oxford Street turned to get into Shaftesbury Avenue so that he could cut across Regent Street and reach Burlington Gardens.

He was driving slowly past the rear of the Royal Academy when he saw her. She was pacing the pavement before the entrance to the arcade. She looked like her photos only in miniature somehow, probably because she was trying to conceal her face in the collar of her dusty-gold tweed coat that highlighted the pale quality of her ash-blonde hair worn down to her shoulders.

When he stopped and waved, her gaze swung to him, and she came running. He opened the door beside him and she settled low in the passenger seat. She kept the collar of her coat well up around the lower half of her face with her left hand, so that her warm brown, golden-flecked eyes peered at him with an expression in their depths he could not be sure about. He thought it was fear, which seemed ludicrous.

She said in a throaty whisper, 'Drive on—quick!'

He decided she was indeed scared, but said nothing until he was approaching Oxford Street, and then he asked, 'Where are we going?'

From the depths of that coat collar beside him came the words, 'Anywhere so long as we won't be over-heard.'

He swung left and saw the lights before the Marble Arch change ahead and settled into the near-side lane between a taxi and a bus.

'How about on the pull-in in front of the Serpentine?'

'In Hyde Park?'

Only someone who wasn't a Londoner would have asked.

'Yes. So just relax till we get there.'

He gave his attention to the road ahead while he felt her studying his profile. He was mildly annoyed that it wasn't more impressive, and had to force himself to stop wondering what the hell she was thinking about him. As though it mattered a damn.

He cut into the park when the lights changed and

took the curving sweep west that finally brought him bearing left again towards the sheet of water with the sun playing on it and gilding its surface with spangles of brightness.

'There's a lovely lake in London,' she began humming until she was sure of the words, and as he nosed into a space facing the water, braked, and cut the engine she finished with, 'The dear old Serpentine.'

'Well, that's it,' he told her. 'Take a good look if you want to, and if you're feeling warm remember that hardy characters dive into it on Christmas morning, even if they have to break the ice. Of course, you could undo your coat.'

She pulled herself higher in her seat, picked her handbag from the floor and placed it over the glove compartment, so that anyone passing in front of the car would not have a clear view of her face, and then pushed her chin clear of her coat collar and shrugged her shoulders loose.

'Now,' she said. 'I suppose I'd better tell you. By this time the police will be looking for me.'

Capper nodded sagely and pursed his mouth, giving the impression that he had something to think about.

'You don't look lost to me, Baroness.' Until that moment he hadn't been sure what he was going to call her.

He discovered he still hadn't been sure, for she said, 'Please, no title. Let's settle for Elise.'

Well, it wasn't her real name, but he was ready to settle for it. Before he could speak again she added, 'I believe you're Mike. Well, don't think I'm worried about the police looking for me. They can't do more than send me to jail.'

He shot her a sideways glance and decided that she wasn't being arch or funny or anything else suggested by her words. The shadow of that scared look remained in the dusky depths of her lovely eyes.

'So it's not the police,' he said. 'Then who is it?'

'Andy.'

He had to think about it for a long moment before deciding he had to be sure.

'Andy Beecham?'

'Of course. But he may not go to the police. You can never be sure with Andy.'

'That's his reputation,' he agreed drily. 'It's said to make life difficult for a lot of people.'

'And now I'm one of them,' she assured him.

'You can be sure of one thing, Elise,' he said gravely. 'The police are not after you, or if they are they weren't told to find you by Andy Beecham. He's someone who always—repeat always—takes care of finding people he wants to find without asking a favour from the police. He has plenty of persons who will do that for him. The rumour on the Rialto is that he pays them handsomely. There is also another rumour that is gaining currency. This is that he expects to marry you sometime before long.'

She nodded slowly, as though digesting his words, and came up with something quite shattering.

'Is that why you want to write the series about me for the *Daily Signet*?'

'No. I want to write the series because they're going to pay me. If I fall down on the job I don't get paid.' Capper swung half round to look at her and found himself still liking what he saw. 'Now, if we can consider these introductions sufficient, will you tell me why Beecham is after you.'

'Because I've got the tape. I took it.'

Her tone and manner implied that he would understand what she was talking about.

'You're telling me you've stolen a tape from Andy Beecham?'

'I don't call it stealing.'

'That's rewarding. Just for my peace of mind, what would you call it?'

'Precisely what I told Andy I called it.'

Capper sighed. He began to see that they were not on the same wavelength in this matter of a tape's ownership. Nor was the lovely Baroness Rorthy, or whatever she chose to call herself, being very helpful or even explicit.

Suddenly she too turned half round to face him, so that they were only inches apart and staring at each other when she said, 'Let's see if I can make you understand.'

Capper wanted to lose his temper. She was implying that he was stupid or thick even if she didn't realize it. But he thought of Tom Valence and forced himself to say quietly, 'That would help. I should like to understand what you've done and why we're here and also what I'm expected to do about it—if anything. I want to write a series about you for an editor who wishes to publish it, which is nice as far as it goes. But I can't very well use a typewriter if some of Andy Beecham's goons come calling and smash my fingers just to let me know how much their boss disapproves of my behaviour. Or even yours, Elise.'

'You're not frightened of Andy's Press reputation as

a shadow man behind the London underworld, surely.'

'I'm shaking in my shoes, and I feel I've every reason to, so please come to the point, Elise.'

'Well,' she said, turning to look at some boats on the surface of the lake, 'Phil has these gambling debts.'

'Phil?'

'My brother, of course.'

'Of course,' he agreed, suddenly aware that he knew almost nothing about her except what everybody else in Britain had read in the newspapers or heard on the radio and TV.

'I told Andy not to give Phil credit and he said he wouldn't.'

'But of course he did.'

'Of course.'

The dialogue was threatening to become cosy. To prevent such a disaster Capper said, 'You mentioned a tape, I believe.'

'I'm coming to that, Mike. You must be patient.'

'I really must,' he agreed, not speaking to her.

'Andy gave Phil credit in order to bring what he thinks of as pressure to bear on me. You follow?'

'It's a very old device, Elise.'

'I'm sure it is. But Phil came to me and said he had been played for a sucker.'

'That isn't new either.'

'I told him not to be a fool and to stop going to these gambling joints. But he said he had a way of making the crooks pay. Yes, Phil's words. Making the crooks pay. So he went to see Andy, promised to pay up if given a little time, and was told to take all the time he wanted. But when it came time to go he didn't. He hid himself with a miniature recorder, and that's how he came to get this tape of Andy talking to someone who represents the Mafia.'

Capper caught his breath, let it go slowly, and only then trusted himself to swear. He apologized.

'That's all right. I said worse, Mike, when he came and told me what he had done. He said he was not only going to clear his gambling debts with the tape, but earn what he called expenses.'

'Other people might call it blackmail.'

'I don't want to think Andy would call it that.'

'He's probably got a much tougher word.'

She thought about it and nodded. 'You may be right. Anyway, someone robbed Phil of the tape after burgling his flat, and later said on the phone he'd be smart to forget it, as Andy didn't know who had taken it. But Andy was paying to buy it. You follow?'

'I'm ahead of you, Elise. The caller gave no name and no explanation of how he came to know of the tape's existence. But he succeeded in scaring off your brother, who came back to you to get him back his plaything. Did you tell him you'd try?'

'No. I said I would. But now I've decided not to hand it back to Phil.'

'Sounds like you've seen the light, Elise.'

'I think so, Mike.' She reached for her handbag, opened it, and took a cassette from the main pocket. 'Here, I'm giving it to you. So now you know why I'm suddenly scared of Andy. I went to his place when he was out, found the tape in the drawer of his desk with the spring lock he showed me how to open, and you know what that means?'

'Andy Beecham's already paid handsomely for the tape,' Capper said miserably and caught it with his left hand as she tossed it to him. He stared at the small spool wound on black plastic. 'You know what will happen to me if I run it through? I'll be found at the end of some dark alley and taking no further interest in this life.'

'Don't be so melodramatic,' she chided.

'Come to think of it,' he reflected aloud, 'that might happen to me if I don't run it. Because Beecham will know, won't he, who took it?'

'I'm afraid so.'

'And when he finds who picked you up outside the Burlington Arcade someone will come looking for me, won't they?'

'It could happen if he gets mad. Yes, Mike, I'm afraid it could,' she said seriously. 'That's why we're leaving London. So please let's be on our way. Make for the nearest bridge over the Thames and on the way I'll tell you where we're going.'

Capper stretched out a hand to turn the key in the ignition, paused with fingers extended, and asked, 'Why should I do this crazy thing?'

She looked at him. Her lovely eyes were wide with genuine surprise.

'I thought you wanted my story for that newspaper editor. You do, don't you?'

Capper swallowed hard and turned the ignition key. On the spur of the moment he couldn't think of a more eloquent answer.

CHAPTER TWO

Capper had crossed Albert Bridge and was snaking his way across Battersea when he said, 'You seem to have got one thing wrong about me.'

'Oh,' she said, not making it into an exclamation. 'What?'

'I'm not a detective.' She said nothing, and for the record he said, 'I'm a freelance journalist.' She still sat wordless, as though silence really was golden, and at today's rate for Kruggerrands was not to be destroyed. So he pushed what he thought was his advantage. 'Another thing, Elise. You said a while back that you had told Andy. I took you to mean you had told him you had taken the tape. Was I right?'

She nodded and watched the people on a pedestrian crossing as though she had to memorize their faces.

'Why?'

'I didn't want him to think I was a thief.'

'You mean, you went to his place where you're accepted, took the tape from that secret drawer in his desk, and when you left you phoned him, wherever he was, and told him what you'd done.'

They were over the pedestrian crossing and picking up speed. He became aware of movement by her, looked at her, and saw she was shaking her ash-blonde hair in a slow negative. It was like a mimed drawl.

'No, I don't mean that, Mike. I didn't know where he was. I scrawled a few words to tell him who had taken the tape and left them in the secret drawer.'

'I see. By that time you hadn't decided to phone me?'

'You hadn't entered my mind. Why should you? We had an appointment fixed for tomorrow morning at ten-thirty.'

'That's what I thought. I've even got your address in my pocket.' He tapped his wallet and received a sweetly professional smile from someone who knew how to behave before a camera, especially when a close-up was being taken. 'So what changed your thinking?'

'Well, it was this sound,' she said gravely. 'And the smell of the cigar. Andy doesn't smoke cigars, neither do his servants. But someone was smoking a cigar. The smell was fresh, and it hadn't been outside the room when I entered it.'

'But it was when you left?'

'Yes. I can trust my nose, Mike. In fact, I can trust all my senses. I've had to, you see.'

'Including your hearing. You did mention a sound.'

'I did. It was the squeak of shoes on the feet of some-one trying to move quietly and not making too good a job of it. You know what that made me think? This someone had watched me go into the room, had tried to spy on me, and then didn't want to be seen by me when I left.'

'And that's something you can't explain?'

'Worse than that. It scared me. I suddenly wanted to get away. I mistrusted what I had got myself into.'

When he remained silent in his turn she said, 'Well?'

'I'm thinking that was the first sensible decision you've come to in a long time.'

Woman-like, she countered with, 'What about agree-ing to meet you and talk about the series?'

He looked at her again, his eyes brooding and moody.

'Maybe I'd feel better if this was ten-thirty tomorrow morning,' he said, 'and the rest of today was something that hadn't happened.'

'My God, you have got cold feet,' she accused, as though she felt she could be more cheerful with the miles behind them building up steadily. 'I'd like a cigarette if you're not afraid to smoke.'

He lit two cigarettes and gave her one and watched Wimbledon on one side, and Roehampton on the other, flow past. The butts had been tossed from the windows and Esher's bottleneck was compelling the Capri Ghia to crawl when Capper said, 'I'm still waiting to learn where we're headed.'

She opened her handbag, repaired the minimal damage done to her lips by smoking the cigarette, and shut the bag with a firm click.

'Churstead. It's not far south of Farnham. Very pleasant country, rather like Sussex around Midhurst and towards Chichester. I've got the house Josef left me. My country home if you like. It's about three miles south of Churstead on the Hindhead road. The place is called Little Mere. It has a patch of water at the edge of a bluebell wood, and in spring you have a wonderful view from my bedroom window, with the blue mist of the bell flowers merging with the fresh green of the trees, and—'

The Capri Ghia seemed at that moment to develop a mind of its own and wobble on the road.

'You've got too much alcohol in your petrol,' she said, and laughed, but broke off the sound as the wobble increased until Capper braked.

'A blow-out,' he said. 'Must have done some damge

because these tubeless tyres are pretty good and let you down very smoothly. But this isn't a normal occasion, is it?'

'What's that supposed to mean, Mike?'

'I think I've got a lady hoodoo aboard.'

He got out, stared at a flat rear wheel, and came back to the open door on the driver's side of the low-slung car.

'I'll have to change it. Then I'll want a garage to repair the damaged tyre. I can't afford to risk lightning striking in the same place twice.'

'You should cultivate a healthy superstition.'

He grinned at her in a way that heightened the colour in her cheeks and gave a new polish to the brown-gold eyes.

'Just don't tempt me, lady.'

Three garages where he called said they couldn't repair the tyre until the next day. The fourth agreed to repair the tyre if he could wait for half an hour before the work was started. This was the garage where the works foreman told him the tyre had been chewed up by slivers of broken bottle glass.

'You're lucky the glass didn't slice through the walls,' he told Capper. 'Get that sort of damage to a tubeless and it usually means a new tyre.'

When he reported back to his passenger she decided that they might turn back to the tea-shop they had passed.

They spent three-quarters of an hour over a light meal, went back to the garage to find the tyre was being worked on, and had to wait another half-hour. By the time Capper was again on his way he had lost most of three hours. When he put his foot down he was told,

'There's no need to hurry. We've plenty of time, and I can put you up for the night with no trouble.'

So he cut his speed to a modest forty and gave fresh thought to the situation into which he was travelling. He decided it might impress Tom Valence if he gave the news editor a ring from Little Mere and announced where he was and with whom. The sun was losing altitude noticeably by the time he was through Churstead, and slowing for the turn that led to the house she had described as 'Off to the right through the woods.'

The track wasn't a normal motor road and had no metalled surface, but plenty of dips and potholes which tested the car's springs and torque.

'Through there.'

She pointed to a pair of white wooden gates, both of which were pegged back with staples. On the top rail of the left gate was the black-painted word 'Little' and in a similar position on the right one was 'Mere'. They had arrived.

Capper turned between the gates, wheels churning the surface stones of a gravelled drive. He drove along a curving avenue of shrubs and trees that had been kept trimmed and pruned. When he saw the red-brick shape of the house looming at the end of the twin rows of trees his gaze became both fixed and appreciative.

'Queen Anne, I'd say, from the chimneys and windows,' he decided. 'Very easy to look at and doubtless pleasant to live in if you don't demand central heating.'

'Or even if one does,' she told him quietly, as though sight of this possession never failed to impress her.

'Josef had the place modernized, as he put it. Of course he wasn't referring to the architecture.'

Capper braked. As he did so a thought occurred to him.

'You've got your key?'

'Naturally.' The single word was mildly reproving.

She opened the door beside her, swung her legs on to the drive, and rose elegantly from her seat, at the same time feeling for the clasp of her handbag. She was doubtless about to produce the key that would open the wide front door for them. However, she was saved the necessity.

She was still reaching into her handbag, and Capper was walking around the car to join her where she stood with her hand plunged into the bag, when the front door of the house named Little Mere opened. Standing framed in the opening was a man of medium height. He wore a short car coat of russet-dyed sheepskin with a collar that looked like mink. He had a full head of curly dark hair streaked with grey that gave his rather ordinary-looking face of indecisive features a bogus look of distinction. He stood there staring at the woman. After one quick stabbing look at Capper his gaze remained on Josef Rorthy's widow. He didn't bother to take his hands from the coat pockets into which they were thrust.

Capper felt his jaw muscles slacken with surprise. He tightened them and ground his teeth. If he was in any doubt as to the identity of the man who had opened the door and stood awaiting their arrival the woman's first words removed it.

'Why, Andy,' she said, sounding more amused than genuinely surprised. 'Fancy you getting here before me.'

She turned to Capper, whose jaw was aching under the punishment given it. 'Isn't that really something, Mike? No one could call Andy a dawdler and be telling the truth.'

She closed her handbag, tucked it under her arm, and walked to the door, watched each step of the way by Andy Beecham, whose face was deadpan, giving away nothing of his feelings. Capper followed her, slowly overtaking the slim figure in the tweed coat with shoulders braced as she almost sauntered. Capper was only a couple of paces behind her when she halted. That was when the man in the sheepskin took his hands from his pockets. The right reached forward, and for an instant Capper thought he was about to take a slam on the jaw.

But Beecham's fist was not closed. His hand came down on Capper's shoulder, and the open fingers gripped hard, pinching like the teeth of a spring trap.

'All right, Mike, or whoever the hell you are,' he said in a voice that reminded Capper of gravel being churned in a concrete mixer, 'don't get shy. I'm here to talk, and I've come a long way. Disappointments could upset me. They might do more than that to you.'

As though to emphasize his words, the speaker bore down on Capper's shoulder. The journalist tried ducking to avoid the pressure, slipped, and stumbled. He went on his knees and dropped his hands to prevent sprawling on his face and belly. Finding himself on his hands and knees, in a grotesque attitude of supplication, he swore.

The woman spoke, and her amusement sounded genuine.

'You do look funny down there, Mike.' She gave a

short sound of spilled laughter. 'Doesn't he, Andy?'

Before Beecham's extended right hand could grab him again Capper pushed himself back on to his feet. He overdid it in his haste and nearly went over backwards. He stood rocking as he strove to recover his balance. It was Beecham's hand that steadied him.

'You drunk, feller?' he asked, withdrawing his hand.

He didn't wait for a reply, but turned and walked into the hall.

'Close the door after you, Mike,' said the woman before following Beecham.

Capper brushed his hands together and again followed her. He closed the front door and walked down the hall and into a comfortable lounge where a gas fire in a large grate burned under simulated logs. It was the sort of room that two hundred and fifty years before had been called a withdrawing-room, and a mere century earlier had been known as a drawing-room.

Beecham was standing with his back to the warmth in the hearth as the woman relaxed in a chair to one side of it.

'You know how to make yourself at home, Andy,' she said.

'It's a gift.'

'Not from me.'

Both paused, eyeing each other.

'Where's Ruth?' she asked.

'If she's your maid, she ran upstairs and locked herself in her room.'

Capper grunted. 'Nice to know some female around here shows sense.'

Beecham shook his head. 'Don't tempt me, Mike. I

want you conscious. So co-operate, huh?' He stroked his folded right fist with his left hand. 'O.K., huh?'

For answer Capper sat down in the chair on the other side of the hearth. In truth, his mind was elsewhere, as they say. He was wondering if the woman had known what to expect when they arrived, and if so how and why? Just as he realized that the answers would not be readily forthcoming. Which didn't make him like a situation he felt was bad and growing worse.

He had an idea how much worse when Beecham folded his arms, walked away from the grate four paces and turned about to face the seated pair and say, 'Where's the cassette?' He looked at the woman, then at Capper, and then returned his gaze to the woman's smiling face. 'Don't play games, and don't try to con me.'

Capper, who wasn't feeling so comfortable at that moment, looked at the woman in whose home he found himself. He expected to see some show of concern on her lovely face now she was confronted by a man who could hide his anger commendably well, probably from long experience of doing so. Instead, Baroness Rorthy seemed sunk in reverie and smiling to herself.

She said, 'Did you come alone, Andy?'

Beecham shot her a puzzled under-the-brows look.

'Of course. But you didn't.'

She smiled. 'Observant of you, Andy. I couldn't, could I? I'd just hired Mike.'

Capper had no liking for her choice of words. For one thing, they didn't fit the facts. He felt like protesting, but when he encountered the new speculative look directed at him by the other man he bit back words he might afterwards have regretted. What threatened to become a painful hiatus was relieved by a loud slamming sound from somewhere in the upper regions of the old house. The two men tensed visibly while the still relaxed woman smiled.

'Only Ruth,' she told them. 'She's not young. After all, what young person would bury herself out here? She's middle-aged, married, and keeps to herself. She isn't good company, and prefers not to meet strangers. Says she's had her fill of them.'

'Where's her husband?' Beecham queried.

'In jail.'

'So she's serving a sentence too.' It just managed not to be a sneer.

'Put it that way if you like. As I said, she's not young. Anyway, she suits me and I was glad to hire her.'

'Like Mike here?'

She ignored that and put a question of her own.

'What's happened to Phil?'

'Let's forget him for the moment. No more side-tracking.' Beecham's voice hardened. The churning gravel was solidifying. 'My cassette?'

He held out a hand and took a pace forward. Capper prepared himself to bound from his chair.

'I haven't got it now, Andy. You should realize that.' She sounded mildly reproving, as though the other had been guilty of some stupidity.

Beecham's gaze swung again to Capper.

'So he's got it.'

The way he said the words made Capper feel numb. The feeling stopped spreading when the woman laughed lightly and said, 'You catch on quickly, Andy. I gave it to him and then dragged him all the way here, so that you could take it from him. Now that really would be playing games.'

'Not with me, sweetheart.'

He seemed to leap at her and grapple with her left wrist to imprison it all in one smooth motion. A quick look of surprise—or was it pain?—crossed her face, but her lips compressed. No sound spilled from them.

'All right, Elise,' Beecham growled. 'You know how I feel about you, but don't exploit it, darling. I wouldn't like that and it might turn me nasty. And believe me, I can be very nasty if I'm turned on. So don't overplay your hand.'

He released her wrist. It fell to her lap.

'Why is the tape so important?' she asked.

'If you knew that you could be in real danger,' he told her, 'and not from me.'

Watching her, Capper was sure she shivered. He felt the numb feeling returning.

She said, 'Phil says he was played for a sucker. I believe him.'

'Well, believe me, too, Elise. It was a mistake or misunderstanding. Call it anything you like. I wasn't even there when he got in over his ears. I had given orders that he wasn't to be encouraged. My words were taken the wrong way. Not encouraged to walk away with a big wad in his pocket. But when he continued losing that was deemed to be O.K. Afterwards he got mad and came storming in to see me. You know that. I've told you already. Then he took advantage of my invitation to come back when he'd cooled off and we'd talk it over. After all, I'd got you to think about.'

She opened her red mouth to speak sharply, but closed it silently, though her breathing was suddenly hard and her breasts rose and fell more noticeably.

'You decided I'd be easy if you had a money hold on Phil.'

The man bending over her shook his head. 'Not so, and not my style. If I couldn't get you just by myself, I wasn't wanting to get you on the crook. You're not just another piece of woman. I've told you. You're *the* woman, the one and only. All right.' He gestured, throwing his arms apart. 'So I'm in love with you. That's not exactly news to you, damn it.'

Her breasts were still rising and falling in tumult when she turned to look at Capper.

'What can you do with such a man, Mike?'

By this time the resentment he had been holding back overcame the numbness.

'You could marry him,' he snapped.

He was suddenly the beneficiary of four surprised and glaring eyes. Beecham recovered himself first, by which time he had found something humorous in the situation.

'Good advice, and you paid for it, sweetheart,' he grinned.

'What's that supposed to mean?' she retorted.

'Didn't you say you hired Mike?'

Capper decided it was time he made amends. After all, he was investing his time in the woman, and an investment was something one protected.

He produced his Smith and Wesson and levered himself on to his feet.

'I've decided I've no reason to like you, Beecham,' he said, conscious that the woman was sitting very still and staring at him with wide eyes.

All Beecham said was, 'Put that damned thing away or I'll beat your ears off.'

Capper's response was to flick off the safety with his thumb and level the short-barrelled thirty-eight at the russet-dyed sheepskin. If I've got the nerve to squeeze the trigger, he thought, I'll ruin an expensive coat. Then he laughed.

'What's so damned funny?' Beecham demanded.

'I just thought of something. I can't get jailed for shooting a wolf in sheep's clothing, can I?'

Elise Baynard suddenly doubled up. Her laughter sounded like suppressed shrieking.

'It wasn't all that funny,' Beecham complained, looking offended.

'I think we'd better leave,' Capper told her.

'When I know where Phil is,' she said on a new note of doggedness.

'Tell her,' he said, motioning with the gun.

Again there was an interruption. The phone on a side-table across the room rang.

Beecham took a step towards it, only to have the gun in Capper's hand wiggle at him as its owner said reprovingly, 'Uh-huh. Just stay put.'

The woman was at the phone by this time and asking, 'Who is it?' Then she sounded both surprised and angry. 'You want to speak to Mike Capper? Good God! How could you possibly know he's here?' After a pause she said, 'Oh' and held the phone out to Capper. 'If you know a Stella Daly, she wants to talk to you. Says it's important, but she won't tell how she knows you're here.'

Stella!

The woman he had been eager to have change her name to Mrs Capper and take off with him on a honeymoon to the Costa del Sol, the woman he had been trying for more than a year to forget without noticeable success. The woman he had assured himself he would forget but who roamed through his thoughts most nights after he had brushed his teeth.

He took two paces towards the smiling woman holding out the phone invitingly. He could hear the diaphragm crackling. Stella asking if he was there.

He stretched out his left hand to grab the instrument, but he didn't make it.

Andy Beecham, moving with the lithe and fluid motion of a panther in a hurry, reached him first and the swift karate chop on the back of his neck sent him into a deep sleep before he collapsed on the carpet at the exquisitely shod feet of the Baroness Rorthy, who lifted the phone to her face and said, 'I'm afraid he's been unavoidably detained—if you know what I mean.'

Then she hung up.

CHAPTER THREE

When Mike Capper came to and opened his eyes it was
to find himself alone, on the carpet where he had fallen,
with the simulated logs still throwing a too-red glow
across the room, where shadows were invading the corners. His first thought was his gun. He climbed shakenly
to his feet and looked for it.

He didn't find it.

Then he fell into one of the fireside chairs and froze,
although the room was quite warm. Slowly the dull
ache at the back of his neck eased, enough for total
recall of what had happened and that final phone call
which had him removing his attention from Andy
Beecham and giving that fast operator an opportunity
to ring down a quick curtain on the preceding con-
frontation.

Before he could start putting the facts through a
mental sieve his thinking processes were switched by a
sound that slammed into his brain like a hammer beating on a metal tray. A car was coming up the drive.

The only person he thought it could be was Phil
Baynard, whose sense of timing was either very good or
very bad. He decided to make sure, and pushed himself
on to his feet. He stood taking deep breaths and flexing
his arms from the shoulders down, clenching and opening his hands to be sure of his fingers' responses. Then
he hurried into the hall and threw wide the front door
as a pair of headlights washed over him. He dropped
his gaze to stare for a reminiscent moment at a shrub

beside the wide steps where Beecham had first used his hand on him.

The car stopped. Someone he couldn't see beyond the lamps' brightness turned them off and got out. He switched on the hall light.

When he saw the face of the woman who stepped out of the dusk to confront him he felt choked.

'Stella.'

Light-coloured eyes surveyed him gravely. He remembered with a feeling of heat the last time he had kissed them, and the unsmiling red mouth.

'Hallo, Mike.' The same smooth, velvety texture to the words, and yes, there was a faint suggestion of *Je Reviens* clinging to her presence there. 'You're no longer unavoidably detained as the woman said. I thought I'd better see for myself.'

'It was no more than a rumour. Remember what you once said about rumour?'

'I've said a lot of things about rumour in my time,' she admitted cautiously.

But he knew she understood what he meant and the occasion they had been together when she said it. He repeated the words although the swift look that came to her clear eyes told him there was no need.

' "Rumour is the source of my Daly fare." '

He couldn't keep the echo of bitterness from his tone, and he saw her flinch. Then he was surprised to find himself empty of words he wanted to speak. He stood back, closed the door after her, and followed her into the room where he had come to alone.

He switched on more lights, and to break new ice that was forming said, 'Where did you phone from?'

'A call-box this side of Farnham. As you've guessed,

I'm after an interview with the late Baron's widow.' She hesitated and produced cigarettes. 'I assume it was the delectable Elise herself who spoke to me. What happened?'

She chose a cigarette and offered him the pack. He took one and gave her a light, taking time to wonder if she was going to con him again. If he let her it wouldn't sit well with Tom Valence.

'You still a section editor on *Wench*?'

'Assistant editor.'

'Well, it paid you to stay single.'

She blew a cloud of obscuring smoke between them as she eased back in the chair she had chosen and crossed her legs.

'You know how to use words, Mike,' she said quietly. 'You could have chosen a few others that would have made your congratulations sound more sincere.'

'I wasn't congratulating you, Stella.'

'Funny how one never learns some things from experience,' she smiled. 'I'd forgotten what a bastard you could be, Mike, while I'm sure you've remembered what a bitch you believe I am.' She flicked ash into the space behind the false flicker of the simulated logs. 'All right, let's quit kicking each other in the teeth and just share our mutual gratitude for not being married to someone we each don't like. You still haven't told me what happened.'

Capper searched for an ashtray and drew up another chair. He took his time, thinking fast. He put the ashtray on the arm of her chair, where they could both reach it. Then he told her.

She listened without interrupting. Only when he stopped speaking did she say, 'Her brother Phil would be a liability for any sister. At the moment you're involved in something I couldn't touch. Andy Beecham and his gambling establishments aren't for the readers of *Wench*. His most glamorous croupier is, especially as current rumour brackets the lady's near future with several rather stimulating enterprises, none of which would leave her worrying where her next case of champagne and box of caviar is coming from.'

She leaned forward to tap out her cigarette, and Mike again had a choking sensation when he stared at the stretch of exposed neck between the collar of her dark plum-coloured jacket and the crisp curls clinging to the nape. He had intimate memories of that small area of her body.

They were memories he had tried to crowd out of his consciousness and failed. Again he caught a faint whiff of *Je Reviens*.

As she leaned back their faces came close, inches apart, and they looked into each other's eyes with no mask over the expressions. He tried to play it light.

'Very fitting, Stella,' he commended, knowing the words would puzzle her.

'How do you mean?'

'*Je Reviens*. Well, you have returned, but I didn't expect it to be this way, and I bet you didn't.'

Instead of saying anything, she twisted the diamond five-stone ring on the third finger of her right hand with the fingers of her left, which were undecorated. He was intended to draw a conclusion, and obliged by drawing the wrong one.

'So you've got someone else, only you wear his ring on the other hand. Don't tell me I made you superstitious.'

She dropped her hands in her lap and looked at him.

'You bloody fool, Mike.' The words were uttered softly.

He started. 'Hey, let me look at that ring.' Before she could avoid his clutch he had caught her right hand and raised it near his face. 'It is, by God.' He sounded awed. 'That's my ring.'

'You mean the one you gave me. You didn't ask for it back, as I recall.'

'Hell, I don't give things to get them back.'

'Bully for you, buster,' she said coarsely. 'But then I don't take them just to toss them back.'

'But you're wearing it.'

'Don't sound surprised, for God's sake. It was a nice ring. I chose it myself from the jeweller's tray, and I happen to like diamonds. I keep reading they're my best friend.'

He sagged back in his chair.

'You didn't drop the ring in a drawer and forget it.'

'Anything I can do that to I can get rid of permanently,' she informed him, a new bleakness creeping into her voice. 'A nice ring, like I said, so I wear it.'

'Doing so didn't make you give me another sort of ring,' he said, and immediately wished he hadn't said it. The words were too flip. They didn't belong with *Je Reviens* and that look in her eyes.

'Don't think I didn't think about it.' She sat upright. 'Now let's stop drooling about has-beens, Mike. We're both here making strictly business calls.' She gave him time to correct her if she was wrong. He didn't. He was still staring at the ring on her right hand, and she went on, 'Isn't there someone in the house? Don't tell me she lives here alone.'

'A middle-aged maid. Beecham scared her upstairs.'

'That'll be Ruth Bailey, married to a jailbird.'

'Genned up, like always,' he grunted with vague approval.

She looked about to say something but changed her mind. She rose, passed him the ashtray, and said, 'I'll go and find her. See what a woman's touch can do. Stay out of trouble, Mike.'

He watched her go out and close the door. She didn't look back. He had been hoping she would. He rose, looked around the room for the first time with a truly seeing gaze. The ache and stiffness had left his neck. He saw a contraption with glass doors revealing rows of brightly labelled bottles. When he opened the door the container rose to present a small bar, well stocked and with several kinds of glasses and tumblers. There was even an ice bucket.

He dropped cubes into a tumbler and poured Johnnie Walker Black Label over them. He felt Baroness Rorthy, or even Elise Baynard, owed him a stiff drink. He was so sure that he finished it quickly and poured a second. He took a little longer over this one. About thirty seconds.

Then he crossed to the door, opened it and stood listening for any sound of voices that might percolate downstairs. He heard nothing and felt encouraged to return to the front door, which he opened. There was enough light from the hall to show the shrub at which he had stared when Stella drove up. He went down the steps towards it, glanced once behind him, and then stooped and began feeling quickly among the lower leaves. He had to grope about before he found it and withdrew his hand.

His fingers held the tape he had been given. He had dumped it surreptitiously when walking round to join the Baroness, as he thought of her, before they entered the house. If Andy Beecham had felt in his pockets before leaving, presumably with the woman, he would have been disappointed. That is, if he had not been bluffed by feminine guile about unloading the cassette on the man she was bringing to Little Mere.

He turned around and walked back up the steps. He was about to step inside the hall when the familiar voice sounded behind him. Again gravel was being churned in it.

'Stay put, Mike. Just do nothing except hand it over to its rightful owner.'

Capper caught a deep breath, hung on to it as he turned to look over his shoulder. Beecham was backing his words this time with a levelled gun in his hand. Capper's own.

'I thought you'd left,' Capper said after letting out his breath and breathing normally.

'Not without my property. You didn't have it on you, so you'd put it somewhere in a hurry. There weren't many places between your Capri Ghia and the porch, but I thought it best to let you recover it.'

'The Baroness might have had it.'

'The Baroness?' Beecham said mockingly. 'Yeah, I suppose she is, but I think of her as Elise. No, I made sure she hadn't.'

'How, for God's sake?'

'How the hell do you suppose? I frisked her. That's when she became talkative. Told me about Mike Capper, journalist, and what you've got cooking about her. Know something? She didn't go for my slapping you down

38

and leaving you on the carpet like some mat I'd tripped over. She started to bawl me out, so I had to tape her mouth and tie her wrists and ankles. She's a woman with too many ideas. Don't copy her. Hand over the cassette. I've waited long enough.'

'Tell me something. How did you get here before she did?'

'You won't believe how easy that was. I drove down, hid my car when I got here.'

'But how did you know she was coming here?'

'Still easy. I had a phone call.'

'From the Baroness?'

'Hell, no, from Ruth Bailey. Elise phoned her. She phoned me. Couldn't be simpler.'

The speaker sounded just that much smug which Capper found to be encouragement enough. He started to turn, as though holding out something in his hand. The gun's angle of menace dropped. That was when Capper went in close with a driving right fist which seemed to push a hole in the surprised Beecham's guts. He buckled over, momentarily helpless, and a moment was all Capper required to swing his left in a savage hook for the other's jaw. The contact it made sent a shock up the journalist's arm. As Beecham fell back against the lintel Capper tore the gun from his fingers. Then he found the safety was still down. He thumbed it off, watched by the other man, who was making a fast recovery and was again balanced upright on his feet.

'My, the violence oozing from the man,' sneered Beecham between broken gulps of air.

'Turn around and lead the way back to your car,' Capper ordered.

There was a pause long enough for the other to eye him carefully. Beecham shrugged inside his russet-dyed sheepskin and turned about. He led the way down the steps and along the drive with the gun levelled on a lower region of his spine, about a yard distant. There was a side-path that curved between more of the shrubs edging a wide lawn. Backed down the path was a Mercedes sports job with rakish lines.

Beecham walked up to the passenger's side and halted as though he had been jerked on a wire.

'She's gone.'

The words came hissing through his teeth.

The journalist said nothing, but he recalled that Baroness Rorthy had once appeared in an Italian film about air smugglers. She had been forced to make a parachute drop somewhere over the Apennines. He had seen the film, which had been in black and white with English sub-titles. However, he recalled that the way the Baroness had freed herself from tangled 'chute harness had been impressive.

'Did you ever see a film called *Drop into Nowhere*, Beechie boy?' he inquired almost casually.

'I don't like that name,' Beecham growled, 'so watch it. Yes, I saw it.'

'Then you saw how she coped with some tricky parachute ropes with a mountain gale blowing, Laughing Boy. Oh, that's a certain Fleet Street editor's private name for you. So why not laugh, Beechie?'

The baited man swore luridly in a hard whisper.

'She didn't get free without someone helping her. I tied her wrists and ankles and I know.'

'She's a remarkable woman.'

'Shut up. Think I don't know it?'

40

Capper was given no time to answer a question that was more likely than not rhetorical.

Both men were startled by the sound of a shrill scream that came from the direction of the house.

'Stella!' Capper exclaimed, springing back and wheeling about. He heard the other man shouting questions, but he wasn't listening and he wasn't staying to inquire. He was running back along the curving path.

He reached the house and saw the front door open, with the light burning in the hall. Framed in the light was Stella Daly, but he knew as soon as he saw her that the scream had not come from her. It had been torn from the throat of the second woman, grey-haired, scared, who Stella was trying to pacify and calm.

The second woman was struggling with Stella Daly, who was having hard work to control her. The grey-haired woman heard the running steps of the two men hurrying out of the darkness. She stretched her mouth wide to scream again.

'Shut up, Ruth,' called Andy Beecham. 'You know I hate hysterical women.'

The woman's mouth closed like a trap. There was a look of shock suddenly mirrored on her sallow face.

'Oh, my God,' she said, tugging free from Stella Daly's restraining hands.

Then she gave way to tears.

'And I don't much care for the waterworks either,' said the man beside Capper.

The words sounded sour.

CHAPTER FOUR

Back in the lounge with the gas-fire and mini-bar, Andy Beecham, totally ignoring the fact that Capper was the man with the gun, seemed to take over the proceedings as though he was their organizer. He poured drinks and handed them round, saying to the middle-aged woman, 'Sorry it's not a Guinness, love, but a drop of good Scotch never hurt anyone. It's when the drops come too close together the trouble starts.'

She managed to smile at him, and said, 'Oh, you are a one, Andy,' which caused Stella Daly to stare and Mike Capper to look on in near disbelief of what he heard.

Beecham also produced cigarettes, and when things were as cosy as he could make them he turned to Stella and said, 'All right, what was the screaming all about?'

When he found himself surveyed under a shrewd and cool appraisal Beecham grinned. As though to help the woman he had addressed over a conversational hurdle, he said, 'It was Ruth, wasn't it?'

The grey-haired woman did her best to bury her face in the generous amount of whisky he had poured for her.

Stella said, 'Ruth and I were talking when she suddenly heard a sound which took her out to the window.'

Ruth Bailey looked sorrowfully at her depleted tumbler.

'I have keen hearing,' she told the room in general.

'And you can knock back a glass with the best of them, can't you, love?' Beecham sounded amused.

He rose and poured more whisky into the woman's glass.

'Not just a little water?'

She shook her head.

'Don't see the point of mixing drinks, do you?' He laughed, looked at the other, and, meeting no responsive smiles, straightened his face and said, 'Oh, well,' shrugged, and took another drink from his own tumbler. 'All right,' he went on, 'so Ruth went to the window.'

He looked expectantly at Stella Daly who said as though there had been no interruption following her last words, 'When Ruth reached the window she saw a figure creeping through the grounds. She was sure it was a man.'

'It was,' insisted the grey-haired woman twisting the tumbler round and round in her hands. She looked at the others in turn. There was a hint of defiance in her manner. 'What's more, it wasn't the first time I've seen someone behaving like that.'

'Like what?' Beecham wanted to know.

'Like he was looking for something without wanting to be seen.'

Capper was watching the other man. He thought he seemed shaken by the words, which was puzzling. He couldn't imagine why the words should make any impact on Beecham. On the Baroness perhaps. That made sense of a sort, and she might know why someone skulking in the grounds would be watching the house and those who came and left. But he could think of no reason why Beecham should be concerned by the news.

43

'It was dark,' Beecham pointed out. 'Your eyesight as good as your hearing, Ruth?'

'He had a torch. He switched it on and off, like he was looking for something.'

'You said you'd seen him out there before,' Stella reminded the older woman. 'But are you sure it was the same man?'

Ruth Bailey shook her head and pushed back some loose strands of grey hair that fell across her face.

'No, I'm not sure because I never saw his face clearly,' she admitted. 'But I've seen a man snooping out there in the dark several times.'

'Recently?' asked Beecham.

'One or twice recently.' The speaker seemed to be making an effort to pull herself together. The reason was soon apparent. She squared her thin shoulders, turned her head to face Beecham, and said, 'Matter of fact, I wondered if it was you.'

Beecham said a surprising thing.

'Are you sure now that it wasn't?'

Ruth Bailey's eyes narrowed. 'It wasn't tonight, was it?'

'I can assure you it wasn't,' Capper put in and received a blank stare.

There was a silence that threatened to become embarrassing as it stretched. All save Ruth Bailey found reason to study the glasses they held. Capper was wondering what was the connection between the middle-aged woman servant and Beecham. He was sure the employer and would-be husband of the Baroness Rorthy had been responsible for having the woman installed at Little Mere. Probably as a spy, to judge from his own words.

But why?

44

Capper sensed mystery he could not begin to understand. He had the tape in his pocket, but he was puzzled by what he felt was a wider mystery. This awareness was enough to make him suspicious of Beecham.

Beechie boy, he growled resentfully to himself, you're up to no damned good. The Baroness doesn't need me to tell her that. Then he reflected that the Baroness's own actions required several explanations, and not for the first time since she had phoned his office wondered just how he was being used. It was the only thing of which he was convinced. He was being used. Relentlessly and regardless.

Andy Beecham broke the silence.

'Miss Daly,' he said. 'It is Miss Daly, isn't it? You're not wearing a wedding-ring, though that means little these days. I don't understand what you're doing here.'

Stella lifted her eyes to stare back at him.

'I detect a note of male chauvinism in that remark, but nothing in the words assures me I owe you an explanation.'

Beecham shrugged at Capper. 'You wouldn't say I'm doing too well, would you, Mike? No score at all.'

It was Ruth Bailey who told Beecham what he wanted to know.

'She's a writer. So she told me, Andy.'

Another thing, Capper reflected, she's on first-name terms with Beechie. It must point to something not on the surface.

'Two writers,' said Beecham. 'Both of you after Elise's story?' Receiving no answer, he said more slowly, 'Is that why, Miss Daly, you asked for Mike when you got through, instead of first talking to Elise about coming down here?'

Stella shook her head and brushed flakes of cigarette ash from her plum-coloured skirt.

'Not altogether,' she said and avoided Capper's questing look. 'I wanted to explain something to him before he got a wrong idea.'

'Like crowding his territory?'

She didn't rise to the fresh bait. Instead, she asked, 'What did your mistress say, Ruth, when you told her about the man in the grounds?'

Beecham jerked his head round at that, looked hard at Ruth Bailey, who was staring wistfully at what was left in her glass.

'She said I must have been dreaming.'

'What about her brother?' The words were suddenly shot at her by Beecham.

The hand holding the glass on her knee trembled despite the tight grip of her fingers, revealed by the whiteness of her knuckles.

'I haven't seen Mr Baynard,' she mumbled, 'not for weeks.'

'Did he live here at one time, Ruth?' asked Stella.

'He might have. He used to come down here, but never stayed long. I believe he's got a place of his own in London.'

The words were still offered in a mumbling tone.

Capper looked at the other man. Ruth Bailey's knuckles were not the only white ones in the room. Andy Beecham had his hands crossed and gripping his wrists. He made a visible effort to relax and turned to the servant.

'Ruth, can't you make us some tea or coffee? We've all been under some strain.'

46

Curiously Ruth Bailey chose to look at Stella, who gave her an encouraging smile.

'I'm sure your mistress would like us to have a warm drink, Ruth, and perhaps some biscuits. You could manage that?'

'I'm not too good at making coffee. More at home with instant.'

'Then a cup of tea shouldn't be much trouble.'

'Trouble!' Ruth Bailey exclaimed softly, rising and setting down her glass. 'Some people don't know what the word means.' She walked to the door. Before opening it she said, 'But I do. I know what bloody trouble means all right.'

Her exit was made hurriedly.

Capper found Stella looking at him as though expecting a reaction from him. He wasn't sure what she wanted from him, but was very sure what she wanted from Andy Beecham.

He said, 'I think our mutual friend here got Ruth installed. As a spy, is my guess.'

Neither of the others took any notice of the words. Capper finished his drink in a hurry. He felt he had been let down without knowing how.

Stella asked, 'Could I have another cigarette, please?'

Beecham hastened to supply one with a light. As she was savouring the first draw she said, 'You're the notorious Andrew Beecham, owner of a chain of casinos and mystery man of the underworld. You're not what I expected.'

The man shook his head, grinning.

'Don't try to con me. You may get Elise's story, but mine's not in the market. Remember one thing. I have

47

good lawyers. I pay them well to keep journalistic mud from sticking. So be warned, lady.'

'You've no liking for the media?' she challenged.

'Not when they presumably turn up for an interview or whatever with a gun in a pocket.'

He didn't look at Capper, but she did, and her eyes were very wide.

'What's the man mean, Mike?'

'It means,' Capper told her, 'that even when he lifted my gun from my pocket he still couldn't keep the Baroness in his car. She got away.'

'Someone helped her, damn it,' Beecham grunted.

'So you say.'

'You men,' Stella complained. She took several fast drags at her cigarette before sitting upright. 'I've got it! The prowler in the grounds. He came prepared with a torch and he was searching, Ruth said. Of course he was. He was the one who found our missing hostess. Where do you think she's gone?'

'To find the police if she's got any sense,' snapped Capper.

'I'm the one the police should listen to if they're interested in the truth,' Beecham muttered.

'Oh, they'd like the truth and they'd listen,' Capper promised him. 'Probably get it all down in quadruplicate and ask you to sign each copy. Then they'd lose you in a cell, where even lawyers only arrive on visiting days.'

'Not very funny, chum.'

'Stop it, you two,' said Stella, like an aunt reproving a pair of young nephews. 'If either of you has anything to say, tell me what it is you're both being careful to say nothing about. I've got a feeling there is something.

It could be the reason the Baroness, as Mike keeps calling her, isn't with us at the moment. He brought her expecting to finalize a deal that would give Tom Valence of the *Daily Signet* a popular series.'

'How do you know?' Capper demanded roughly.

'I met Tom at a recent editors' lunch. Seems his spies had brought him news of the Baroness's recent activities. He wanted information and he sounded like a man checking. As I was fishing in the same pond, I traded some of what I knew for what he would tell me. After all, if he had you writing up the lady, it was in the interest of both of us to make sure *Wench* came up with something very different. On the other hand, if the *Daily Signet* and *Wench* chose to run their Baroness Rorthy features at the same time, it could make for increased public interest.'

'*Wench*, is that the magazine you work for?' shouted Beecham. 'It's full of lies and smears. I'm surprised anyone buys it. Now you've told me, I'll make damned sure Elise doesn't contribute a single word.'

'To do that you'll have to find her,' Stella pointed out.

'I'll find her,' Beecham promised, 'and when I do she's going to learn a few things the hard way.'

'More male chauvinism. I can use that later.'

She was about to add something else, but the door opened and Ruth Bailey entered with a tray of tea-things and a selection of biscuits.

'There's hot water in the jug,' she said, putting down the tray.

'Only three cups, Ruthie,' Beecham pointed out.

'That's right,' said the grey-haired woman. 'I've got a headache and I'm going to rest up on my bed. Baroness

49

Rorthy knows about my headaches and is sympathetic.'

'I'm sure she is,' Beecham grinned. 'I told her they come at odd times.'

The sallow face under the stringy grey hair acquired such a look as might have marked an early Christian martyr about to test at first hand the appetite of the Coliseum's lions.

'As long as she knows,' she managed with a trace of defiance, 'then that's all right, isn't it?'

She started a retreat to the door. On the way she collected the bottle of whisky from the top of the mini-bar.

'Quite a remarkable recovery,' Stella observed as the door closed again. 'Only minutes ago she was screaming in her room overlooking the grounds at the back and ran out and down the stairs. I didn't catch her until she reached the front door.'

'So this someone she saw was at the back of the house?' Beecham asked.

'Of course.'

'But you didn't see him?'

'She ran past me and out of the room towards the stairs before I had time to reach the window.' Stella glanced at Capper. 'I decided I'd better stop her screaming and also prevent her from leaving the house, which she seemed bent on doing. I suppose I can now leave looking after her to the whisky.'

'You're convinced she saw someone?' Capper asked.

'If I had any doubt the screaming convinced me.'

'Look,' interrupted Andy Beecham. 'We're wasting time.' He watched Stella pouring cups of tea, took one from her, and shook his head at the biscuits. 'We're all here for one reason. Elise, and she's gone. Right?'

Capper swallowed some of the tea he had been passed and afterwards half a biscuit which was too sweet for his palate.

'You got a proposal?' he asked warily.

'Yeah. We don't ring the police—yet.'

'You mean we might have to later?' Stella asked, putting down her tea and remaining standing as she nibbled a biscuit thoughtfully.

Capper watched her face in profile, appreciating the clean line of chin and neck, the oval of the face with the fairly high cheekbones seeming to emphasize the trim brows and height of the forehead set in the soft curls across her head.

'Give me a day to decide, Miss Daly. Or may I too call you Stella?'

She shrugged, bit off another piece of biscuit.

'Why should we?'

Capper was gratified that she had included him.

Beecham didn't have to think about his answer. 'Two reasons mainly. I think she could be in danger, and I want to make sure and, if necessary, do something about it. Also, you both want a story from her. Well, if you think you can get what you want by being obstructive, you've got to think again. Both of you.'

'The man's got something, Mike.'

'I know. A crawful of gall, wanting us to give him a day's grace before telling the police the Baroness has vanished.'

'Did she tell you to notify the police when you brought her from London?' Beecham asked, standing with shoulders hunched in a boxer's pose.

Capper started, and knew both the others saw the surprise overtake him. Elise Baynard had been in fear

51

of the police stopping her from whatever she had planned to do with the tape she had confiscated. It wasn't quite the right word. Stolen would be simpler and probably more truthful.

'So she told you the opposite, huh?' It was like having a verbal left hook thrown in his face. He couldn't duck. He could only retreat.

'Go to hell,' he muttered, and didn't feel any better when he saw Stella smiling in understanding.

'He didn't say, Mike, to be fair, he wanted the time before we went to the police. The word he used was decide. But he was careful not to explain what he wished to decide.'

'Thank you, Stella, for nothing.' Beecham managed a grin, but he had a job keeping it pinned in position. 'I want the time because I've got to make inquiries so I can convince Elise she's got no hope of staying alive unless she marries me.'

Stella's very kissable mouth firmed into a thin compressed line as her gaze widened.

'You're asking rather much on trust,' she observed, looking for the first time worried and dubious.

'Mike's got the proof in his pocket.'

That turned her about to stare again at Mike.

'I'm not only confused,' she said. 'I'm scared. Something's happening that I know nothing about. I don't care for the feeling that gives me.'

Mike took his hand from his pocket. It didn't hold the tape he had recovered from the bush, as Beecham plainly expected. It held the Smith and Wesson.

The other man became angry.

'Damn you, I don't like guns and violence. That's the reason I want time. I mistrust violence. It gets no one nowhere except into a hole in the ground if one's unlucky.'

'Well, you've just run out of luck, Beechie. So haul off. Stella and I are leaving.'

'You bloody fool.'

Beecham started to walk towards Capper, who said, 'Stop or I'll put a bullet in your thigh.'

He aimed the short-nosed weapon at the advancing man's right leg.

'Bluff,' sneered Beecham.

'I mean it.'

But Beecham didn't stop. Aware that Stella was holding herself rigid, like someone who knows a miracle is not going to happen, Capper squeezed the trigger. There was a dull click, not very loud, as the hammer of the gun fell on an empty chamber. He fired again, with the same result, and the truth hit him like a physical blow.

'You bastard! You emptied the chambers.'

Unfortunately he had used up his time margin by releasing his anger in words. When the blow Andy Beecham threw at his head came hurtling like a rocket through space his reflexes were too slow. He tried to get his head out of the way, but had time only to turn his chin, so the fist caught him on the side of the jaw.

For the second time he dived at the carpet and fell at a pair of female feet.

Stella sighed heavily as she looked down at the ungainly heap. She bent low and picked up the gun from where it had fallen from his nerveless clasp.

'Sorry, Stella,' said Beecham, 'but he had to be stopped. He was crowding me.'

'No man is an island, as John Donne said long ago.'

'Maybe not. At least I feel I'm entitled to be a peninsula and refuse to be invaded.'

'A novel slant. If you were staying I could give you an argument.'

Andy Beecham grinned.

'You know,' he said, 'I'm not overfond of the average woman, but I could spare time for you, if I had any. Which you seem to know I haven't.'

'I believed you when you asked for a day's grace.'

'I might need an extension. O.K.?'

'What can I do about it? Ruth Bailey is most likely already snoring and the gun is empty. By the way, whose is it? Just so that I don't guess wrong?'

He pointed to the prone Capper.

'That's how Elise affects some men.'

'You mean she brings out the worst in them.'

'Yes, but don't tell her—or them.'

'Are you sure you believe your own words?'

His face went bleak before clearing and breaking into another of his mocking smiles.

'I should. I'm in love with her, or haven't you guessed?'

He didn't wait to exchange more pleasantries. He hitched the fur collar of his russet-dyed car coat around his ears and walked out of the room without glancing back. She noted that his step was springy. Andy Beecham was a man who kept himself in condition.

She stooped, looking down at Mike Capper while she heard the departing man's steps becoming fainter over the gravel surface of the drive. She started to think about the intruder responsible for Ruth Bailey's screams, but switched her thoughts when she heard the Mercedes sports car turning to dive away into the night.

She stood up.

'Mike Capper,' she said softly. 'Sometimes you can be just a big blundering fool.'

The man hugging the pile of the carpet stirred. He made mumbling sounds. When he sat up Stella Daly was drinking a fresh cup of tea she had poured and was nibbling another biscuit, while observing the return to consciousness with sharply critical eyes.

'Where's that swine Beecham?'

'Gone.'

'With my gun?'

'That's in my handbag. I think it's safer there. You lose it too easily.'

'I was tricked, both times.'

She drank more tea and munched another piece of biscuit.

'Of course. That's expected treatment from a tricky customer.'

He slapped his pockets.

'He's taken the tape, too. And you let him.'

Stella was already wondering if Andy Beecham had remembered his oversight and would come back.

'I couldn't stop him doing what he wanted to. Be reasonable, Mike, and let's hurry. We've each got a car outside, and I feel we ought to be making our separate ways back to London.'

'Why?'

Capper was on his feet testing his jaw with gentle fingers.

'For one thing I missed lunch and these biscuits aren't really satisfying. For another, I've seen enough of Andy Beecham for one day.'

'What about the Baroness?'

'I've a hunch he'll have more luck finding her than we will.'

'I suppose you're right, Stella.' Capper was assailed by a promising thought. 'How about my buying you some dinner. Say in Guildford?'

She was on the point of saying no when she changed her mind and surprised herself.

'Very well. You know the Postboy, off the High Street?' Capper nodded. 'We'll meet there in an hour's time. No, say an hour and a half. That'll give me a chance to make a phone call that's overdue, and you can get the first drink under your belt.'

They left the house in darkness and parted after a single exchanged glance. As they sat in their cars Capper called, 'You go ahead. I'll cover you. Just in case.'

'Very well,' she said and turned the key in the ignition. As she drove off she was keeping her fingers crossed. She still had the tape she had taken from Capper's pocket in the inside compartment of her commodious handbag. She had the feeling she was getting away with something, but no idea of what.

It wasn't a feeling she could enjoy. Largely because she kept thinking about Mike Capper. Things about him she shouldn't be thinking.

CHAPTER FIVE

The meal in the candlelit dining-room of the Postboy
threatened to develop into the kind of anticlimax that
only an impulsive mistake can provide. Capper was
regretting his invitation when Stella Daly said, 'I think
we would do better talking shop, Mike.'

She spoke without backing up the words with a smile.
That left it to him.

He managed a grin. 'Is it such an ordeal?'

'Not the meal. The steak and the Château Latour
were just what I needed. But not the silence.'

Their eyes met. Both knew why talk had died. Neither
was prepared to voice an echo of their mutual past that
might prove barbed and hard to forgive. But she saw
the dawn of a new eagerness in his eyes watching her
from under slightly down-drawn lids.

Before he could frame a plea she added, 'Shop, I
think. It's good safe territory. Otherwise one of us might
stumble, even without knowing it. I don't think we
should risk that.'

He looked at the ring on her right hand as she lifted
a fork to her mouth. The soft light discovered coruscat-
ing flashes of varicoloured fire. He felt a twinge of
sharp regret that was like muted pain.

'I agree,' he nodded. 'No risks. We've got more than
enough lined up for the day after tomorrow.'

'Beecham and the Baroness?'

'They're twin hazards.'

57

After that the shop talk required no effort. He told her most of what had happened to him. But not all. He was, as they both were aware, a journalist talking to a possible rival. What she told him about the cross-talk with Tom Valence was also not the whole story. That fact was something else they shared. She did, however, explain how she came to make the phone call to Little Mere.

'Tom told me he'd been pushing you, and he knew she had this place in the country left her by her husband. "I don't trust her, Stella," he said. "I think she's playing Mike for someone she might use." I asked him how. You know how Tom covers up. This time he didn't complete the cover. He said, "If she inveigles him to go down to Little Mere it'll be to use him. That's certain. Most likely against Laughing Boy." It didn't register at first.'

'His name for Beecham.'

'I had to ask him before he explained. So when I rang her flat and got no answer I called your office, with the same result. I decided to make the trip, but had second thoughts on the way and put through that phone call.'

'But why ask for me?'

'Shock tactics. I've known them work in the past with lovely ladies like our scheming Elise.'

'I was the one who got the shock.'

'I know. I'm sorry. Something must have happened to take Beecham there. I mean, if you hadn't had that puncture, which let him arrive before you, he would still have found you.'

He shook his head. 'I'm not convinced. In the same way I'm not convinced that Elise is really a free agent.'

'How do you mean?'

'Ruth Bailey was obviously planted there, and for one purpose only.'

'Spy for Beecham?'

'I think so. But I think our Baroness is playing with fire. If I was sure what the truth means to her I'd be more certain.'

'What does that mean? I hate to think of you being evasive.'

It was a mild attempt to reach him with raillery. She was surprised when it didn't succeed. She also felt some concern which she was careful not to show.

'If I had that tape I might be able to share a secret with you, Stella.'

'You haven't heard it?'

'No. I was told to mind the damned thing.'

'Then your reference to her truthfulness or otherwise,' she said, picking her words with excessive care, 'must mean that Elise told you something about the tape and what is on it.'

He wiped his mouth with his napkin, put it back on his lap, and fidgeted with the glass holding the remains of his claret.

'Enough to know why Beecham wants it back.'

After that the talk wilted because both had things to consider from different personal angles. They finished the meal, were served coffee and generous measures of Hine in balloon glasses, and smoked Stella's filter-tips.

She was dithering, she knew, which was not in character. Normally she refused to see herself disturbed by being in two minds about anything. But now she found herself hesitating to tell him that the tape of which he had spoken was only inches away, in her bag. Why she remained reluctant to tell him she could not understand. That too bothered her.

More to release the dam blocking her own stream of thought than to ask a question that would receive an answer, she said, 'Why did you suppose he wants a day for those inquiries he mentioned, Mike?'

He waved away a writhing cloud of cigarette smoke and again caught the flash of fires from her right hand.

'I've a hunch he's in danger and knows that danger could engulf both of them.'

'What gave you a clue? Something she said about the tape?'

'Something she said was on it.'

She had been listening attentively and did not catch a note of certainty in his voice. Capper, she realized, was a man playing guessing games with himself and not being happy, which was probably why he didn't succeed in making his words sound reassuring.

'Well, don't hold back,' she urged, keeping her tone light.

'Stella. I'm not sure it's wise to share this with you.'

Capper hesitated, plainly a man debating an issue with himself. She said nothing. This had to be where he confided in her or he didn't. In a way it was a test of confidence. For both of them.

'She said, Stella, the tape she gave me had a recording of Beecham talking to a representative of the Mafia.'

The shock of the words ran through her like an electric current, tingling her nerve ends.

'Oh, my God, Mike. That damned woman is playing this whole thing too damned cute. She's getting us both involved in whatever game she's playing, and she's doing it with the promise of feature stories that will command a high price.' She paused before asking, 'Well, who is going to name the Mafia and get the Special Branch, the C.I.A., and possibly M.I.6 all making the wrong sort of noises? No editor would be such a fool.'

He shrugged. 'That's not an angle I haven't thought about. But you tell me.'

She surprised him by making a display of looking at her watch and remembered that there had been a time when such mannerisms and obvious ploys of hers had amused him and he had encouraged them. But now he felt a faint uneasiness stirring in him. Whatever Stella Daly could truthfully be claimed to be, she was not predictable.

'That's precisely what I'm going to do in less than fifteen minutes,' she told him gravely. 'To fill in that quarter of an hour let's have another cup of coffee and a fresh cigarette. That should help both of us to keep our curiosity in check.'

'Another tipple from the Hine bottle?'

'No. I've enjoyed a good meal and have no wish to spoil it. Besides, I want to keep a clear head.'

'Sounds ominous.'

'Stop fishing.'

After their coffee-cups had been refilled and Capper had lit their cigarettes he said tentatively, 'If I recall, that phone call you said you must make, would that be making a connection, as it were?'

She shook her head. 'Just wait.'

His face puckered. 'I hope to hell you haven't been too clever, Stella.'

Her eyes narrowed against smoke coiling upwards from her cigarette.

'Clever isn't a word I would apply to either of us in this context, Mike. But I confess to playing a hunch, and over the phone I said I was making the call at your suggestion.'

'Well, thank you for telling me.'

She swept on as though he had not interrupted. 'Because something might happen to you. Something not very pleasant, and of course I felt concerned.'

'You what?'

Then he saw she was smiling at the entrance to the Postboy's dining-room. He glanced at the two men revealed in the brighter light from the corridor and choked.

The two men advanced towards the table where Stella was making signals with a raised hand. Detective Chief Superintendent Gary Bull of Scotland Yard and his chief assistant, Detective Inspector Bert Whitelaw, were both old friends of his and Stella's. Bull and Whitelaw had been on the case that almost ended with wedding-bells for the pair at the table.

'I thought you two would have been married and expecting a baby by now,' Gary Bull grinned, and instantly became aware that he had said the wrong thing. 'Oh, sorry if I've put my big foot in it. Well, long time no see, anyway.' He grinned as he and Whitelaw pulled out a couple of spare chairs, sat down at the table, and accepted an offer of coffee with brandy. 'But it had better be good, my friends,' he added with mock severity. 'Bert and I have driven thirty miles from the Smoke just to listen, as I understand.' Stella was shaking her head. 'No?'

'Not quite,' she said. 'First you see. Afterwards you listen, Gary.'

Bull also could remember some of her verbal tactics in the past when she was weaving her own particular kind of spell. He half turned his head towards his left shoulder, the better to eye her askance, and to let her see he was doing so.

Stella smiled with the suggestive sweetness of a toothpaste ad. The observant Whitelaw felt encouraged to say something.

'Seems like the lady's got a surprise for us,' he told his superior in a heavy stage whisper.

It was a good guess.

However, it was an even bigger surprise for Mike Capper when Stella reached for her handbag, opened it, and took the tape from it.

She placed the cassette in the centre of the table, where it became an instant island of focused attention.

'Jesus,' said Capper involuntarily, and he sounded like a man who was badly shaken. The choked feeling was returning to his throat. 'You know what you've done, Stella?'

'No more than we agreed, darling.'

The words hit him harder than Andy Beecham's slammed fist, despite a sweetness that was cloying.

'I think you've made a right balls up, Elise. I said I wouldn't go along with it if you started enjoying yourself, and you did that all right. Telling that woman on the phone Mike Capper was unavoidably detained. Sheer bloody melodrama. And you know I was against the whole clever-clever caper from the start. It wasn't creating Press interest for your story, merely trying shock tactics.'

'Which are always good before a deal is concluded.

63

Seldom afterwards, Andy. You should remember that. My advice to a born loser, pet.'

She could see Beecham was growing damned annoyed with her, and his annoyance could have rough edges that hurt. All the same, she was confident she could handle him. Hell, she had to with Phil getting close to being out of hand. Which was a double danger with so much at stake.

She glanced around the plush living-room of Beecham's Mayfair penthouse, letting her gaze finally settle on the glowering face of the man seated smoking a long thin cigar at the desk from which she had claimed to have removed the tape she had tossed to Mike Capper.

She said, 'That's another of your troubles, Andy. You're against everything on principle. It's the result of being a nobody pretending he's a real somebody. The pretence is transparent to all except you.'

She had decided roughness should be met with roughness. The one sure way to make Beecham back down from a position he had chosen.

He snarled at her. 'I should push my knuckles in your spiteful face. I don't have to take this from you.'

It wasn't quite laughter that bubbled in the back of her stretched throat. But close enough to fool the angry Beecham, before she told him, 'You do if you don't want trouble from Russ.'

He jerked upright behind the desk that, curiously, did not seem an intrusion in a room that was otherwise furnished for relaxation.

'And that's another thing,' he accused. 'You're trying to play me off against Russ Peacock. He's only my manager. I'm boss man.'

'A straw boss, in name only,' she sneered quietly. 'He's been put to run an operation you couldn't handle. Why don't you admit the truth?'

'I do. Russ is in because of Luigi.' He levelled an accusing finger at her. It wasn't quite steady, as she was quick to perceive. 'You brought in Luigi.'

'And why? Because there wouldn't have been anything to operate without him. Except the casino owners in the North and the provinces don't know that—yet. But don't fool yourself, Andy. You're not fooling anyone else who matters, not even Mae and her lush of a husband.'

'You bitch. You enjoy a bloody slanging match, so you can unload your spleen.' He breathed harshly, emotion riding him with savage spurs. 'Well, let me tell you something. Russ Peacock will go bloody cold on you when he learns you've handed out some free lip about talk with the Mafia. That's something he could do without. This buddy-buddy of yours, Mike Capper, could make a right cow of this for him.'

He expected her to look worried. Instead, she smiled.

'Not if he hopes to get a story that will make him real money and show me a writer who isn't attracted by money,' she invited. 'Even the film rights might sell. I've been in films before, and I don't have to remind you.'

He laughed nastily, and blew smoke towards the chair where she sat across from him nursing the remains of a vodka martini she had mixed for herself. Something else that annoyed him. She treated his penthouse as though she was free to come and go as she liked. Just when it suited her, like now, after making the run back from Little Mere.

'Films. God, you're not referring to that box-office

dog you made in Italy when that phony baron you hitched up with sold you for cash to the Eyetie director because you had a special talent in bedroom sports.'

If he had anticipated this would make her blow her lovely top he was disappointed. She pasted a very pleasant smile around her red pouting lips, and showed her white teeth when she said, 'How would a damned fag like you know what a man and a woman do for their pleasure in a bedroom? Read a dirty book?'

The sudden pressure he put on the fingers gripping his cigar broke it to charred ash. He dusted the smouldering remains from his hand and rubbed them out in the big ashtray on his desk topped by a crystal nymph waving aloft the only garment she possessed. He stared at the woman's lovely smiling face with hatred a dark sheen in his eyes. He told himself she had been determined to draw blood right from the moment he walked back from the parked Mercedes sports.

'The sweet bitch I am supposed to be crazy about. She doesn't just spit venom. She vomits it.'

'You didn't even start that piece of hocum on your own. I had to do it after Russ had given his O.K.'

'Did he O.K. your mentioning the Mafia to that bloody writer?'

'He okayed my getting a couple of first-rate writers, both well known in Fleet Street, a man and a woman, and handing them promises on a string. The idea was to keep them dangling so we could come up with some publicity that would focus attention on the casino chain. On that only. The idea was that if they're looking at one thing they can't be staring at two. That should make sense even to Andy Beecham.'

'You mean you sold this notion to Peacock for some

66

reason of your own. Now you're riding high with Luigi he went along with you. That's what makes sense to me. Before long it'll make sense to Russ Peacock.'

'You'd like that, Andy, so you think it'll happen. What you're overlooking is that Russ isn't crazy about having a homo for even a nominal boss, even if he does look distinguished to middle-aged women who've forgotten that the nuts that matter are not cracked by shop-bought nutcrackers. And on the same subject, if you can make the connection, Russ wanted me to give Capper and the woman something they hadn't bargained for, a little extra hinting at a whole lot more. Why? To keep them from sniffing out the real truth.'

Beecham sat back, folding his arms, eyeing her with overt mistrust.

'You've a damned strange way of doing it. How's Capper going to react when he runs that tape?'

'Which,' she reminded him gently, 'you forgot to take with you when you left.'

His mouth compressed. 'That doesn't answer my question,' he pointed out.

'The answer you want is simple. He won't run it.'

'Why not? You've made him curious.'

She gave him another of those sweet smiles he hated.

'One of your troubles, Andy, is you've got a typical fairy's weakness in the top storey. You told me on the way here you saw Stella Daly take the tape from Capper's pocket before you came back to the Merc and we got the hell out of the place.'

He took offence for the wrong reason. 'Damn it, I wasn't lying when I told you what I saw. I sneaked up to the window and the curtains weren't even drawn. There she was bending over Capper where I'd put him on the carpet. She had a hand in his pocket. I saw her take out the tape and put it in her bag.'

'So who'll play it over?'

When he made no effort to reply she went on, 'Not Capper. That's for sure. It'll be Stella Daly, and when she does there's only one conclusion she can come to. Capper's been playing her for a sucker. Which suits me. It'll also suit Russ Peacock when I explain how Capper will be nailed with a lie if he has opened his mouth. There's only one thing he can do. Try to cover up by saying he must have got what I said wrong. It was his mistake. And will she believe him? If I know anything about Stella Daly she's a real hard lady who doesn't know how to be good with deceivers and similar kinds of male chauvinist pigs.'

'So he'll be mad—at you, honey.' He even managed a pinched sort of smile.

'Not for long,' she reminded him, 'if he still wants a series for the *Daily Signet*, and he does.'

There was grudging admiration in the fresh glare he levelled at her as she nonchalantly uncrossed her photogenic legs and hipwalked to the bar, where she poured another vodka martini and stirred it with a glass prong.

'Make mine Scotch,' he growled at her.

She turned, her brows kinked disapprovingly. On the point of making a cutting remark about his lack of manners, which are supposed to make the man he certainly was not, she changed her mind, smiled, and inquired softly, 'With ice? I advise it. You could do with cooling.'

She crossed to the long broad desk with the drink she had poured for him. He took it silently and drank as though he needed that repair work to his *amour propre* which alcohol in stiff jolts usually did for him.

It was an uneasy moment, for after the slanging match both appeared reluctant to continue. Maybe they were considering the score to date and deciding there could be no advantage in deliberately courting a royal row. Besides, as things stood, each needed the other. If only for a short while longer.

She returned to her chair, thoughtful and taking her time. Before she reached it the red phone on his desk rang. The phone with the unlisted number, and she heard him say, 'You took your bloody time, Ruth.'

The words he spat over the wire meant nothing to her, and she waited until he slammed the receiver down angrily.

'You like doing that, don't you?' she gibed gently.

'Doing what, for God's sake?' he demanded.

'Punishing the phone. You couldn't do that with the softer type of push-button instrument. It wouldn't give you the same satisfaction, would it?'

He ignored her words.

'That damned Ruth Bailey has been asleep, sunk in a bloody drunken stupor after hitting the bottle. She woke up to find the place dark and deserted. The Daly woman and Capper were gone, with their cars.'

'Did she say why she went screaming down to the front of the house when she saw someone creeping round the back? Or so she claims.'

'Oh, I know that. She wanted to warn me.'

The woman's eyes widened and she took another swallow from the drink in her glass.

'Real nice of her, Andy, all things considered. And very thoughtful.'

'It was thoughtful all right. Ruth has a habit of thinking things through so she doesn't make a mistake.

She knows I've been paying her a regular sum since Harry went inside.'

'I wonder how thoughtful and appreciative she'd be if she was told Harry is now out.'

She sipped more of the vodka martini, but somehow didn't seem to be relishing it. Maybe she was being too thoughtful in her turn.

'You could try asking your precious Russ Peacock. He's the one with the money bag and playing it cagey. But I could make a guess at his reply.' He saw she was waiting and refusing to be baited. He smiled unpleasantly and added, 'He'd probably tell you it was to keep tabs on Luigi, another of your special playmates.'

He was a little surprised at her reaction. It was something she either couldn't cover or didn't bother to try.

'I don't believe it. You're trying to scare me, Andy. But it won't work.'

He shrugged, drained his Scotch, and ambled to the bar with the empty glass for a refill. His back was to her. And to the door, which he did not see opening silently. She was watching him, working over what he had said. She saw nothing of the gun that appeared round the edge of the door, which stopped opening after four inches. There was a black-painted metal silencer screwed on to the gun's barrel, which lifted until it drew a careful bead on an unaware target.

There were two abrupt sounds like apologetic coughs. Broken glass and ice cubes flew from the bar in several directions an instant before Beecham cried out and collapsed on the floor in the midst of shiny shards of glass and ice.

The pistol barrel vanished and the door closed with a single click.

By then the woman was on her feet, caught in a protracted moment of indecision, the implication of which was stamped on her features, robbing them of their normal attractiveness. Her face was twisted into near-ugliness. She stared from the closed door to the body of the man below the shattered bar. She stopped being motionless and ran to the fallen Beecham.

Stooping, she rolled him over, and caught her breath involuntarily. His eyes opened to stare closely into hers as he winced with a spasm of pain. Down over his face streamed bright fresh blood. It was pouring from under the dark hair with streaks of grey that was now messy.

'Get Russ at the Palace,' he whispered hoarsely. 'Tell him I need a doctor. One who won't report this to the cops.'

To impress on her the urgency, he gripped her hand hurtfully. When his fingers released their hold she saw blood on her flesh and felt strangely soiled.

She straightened, went to the desk, and dialled the Casino Palace, where the night's action was warming up. She stood with the red phone pushed hard against her ear.

'Tell Mr Peacock the Baroness is calling,' she told whoever was at the other end of the wire, 'and I have to speak to him very urgently.'

She waited.

'I see,' she said dully, and replaced the receiver slowly with tense fingers.

Russ Peacock was not at the Casino Palace and no one there knew when he had left or was expected back.

She returned to the crumpled man with a mask of blood covering one side of his head. She didn't share her news with him. Andy Beecham had passed out.

71

CHAPTER SIX

The meeting in Gary Bull's office at Scotland Yard was arranged for ten-thirty. Mike Capper arrived at five and twenty minutes past and waited for Stella, who turned up eight minutes later with apologies for being delayed by the Westminster morning traffic.

Capper, to her quick appraising look, appeared sober but worried and trying not to show it. He was a little too casual without being aware of it.

'Still sore?' she asked, trying to be understanding and not unfriendly.

He shook his head quickly. 'No, not at all. I believe you took a decision, Stella, genuinely thinking it was the right one. I hope it was.'

It was a pretty flattening announcement for any woman's self-pride. It left her with no feeling of accomplishment. But she overcame an impulse to be bruising.

'I didn't want you to veto it for the wrong reason,' she told him.

He refused to be drawn and she felt constrained to add, 'Also, to be honest, I thought that woman was giving you the run-around and found I didn't enjoy the spectacle. Just possibly she had the same treatment in mind for me. So to me it was time to get reinforcements. No more, no less.'

She didn't feel like serving the explanation with a smile. But she made the effort.

'All right,' he said, 'let's go up and find out what the

reinforcements think about things now they've run over that tape.' On the point of showing her to the lift, he hesitated. 'There's one thing, Stella.'

She looked inquiringly at him.

'It might turn out that there isn't a story in this for either of us. Thought I should warn you before you get deeper involved with the law.'

She gave him an uncertain smile, sensing that he had made a real effort to speak his last words.

'It wouldn't be the first time we've experienced disappointment, Mike. We're old hands at playing according to how the cards fall. So let's find out.'

They went up in the lift and found Gary Bull and Bert Whitelaw waiting for them in the former's office, which was only just short of depressing. Bull was standing at a window smoking and looking as though a back tooth was forcing itself on his attention. His assistant was seated at a desk, a cigarette in an ashtray forgotten, going through the entries in a buff-coloured file. It wasn't a thin file and contained sheets of paper covered with typing. The sheets were of several colours.

'Sorry we're late. My fault,' said Stella. 'I got trapped in a couple of traffic jams. If you'd been at the old New Scotland Yard, to coin a phrase, I might have made it. But down here in Victoria Street, with developers' trucks and bulldozers taking up half the road width, it was impossible to do more than crawl. That's when one was moving at all.'

'Forget it, Stella. We know. Bert and I live here.' Bull turned and shared a perceptive look between the new arrivals. Something had happened to them. He was even more sure now than he had been in Guildford. 'There's been another sort of development to consider—but strictly off the record. I must emphasize that.'

Stella and Mike Capper stared back at him. Both nodded their agreement. Each looked puzzled.

'With that understood,' Bull went on, demonstrating that he had finished smoking, 'I've this to tell you. I've heard, and never mind how or from where, that someone gained entry to Andy Beecham's penthouse without ringing the doorbell and tried to put a bullet in his head.'

He went on even as the others were registering surprise and the first glimmerings of consternation.

'It happened, I also know, that that glamorous puss, Baroness Rorthy, was visiting her employer,' he told them wryly. 'Chairs for our visitors, Bert. They've heard enough, I'm sure, to want to sit down.'

Stella and Capper lowered themselves on to the chairs Whitelaw drew up for them between the two desks dominating the businesslike office with cabinets and shelves for files around the walls. Both were eyeing the superintendent uncertainly and not trying to conceal the shock his words had given them.

'Are you able to tell us more precisely what happened, Gary?' Stella asked, her tone implying that she realized anything in the way of further explanation would be a distinct favour.

Bull grinned, aware that the lady was employing one of her considerable stock-in-trade of feminine wiles.

'I can tell you what I think happened,' he said cautiously. 'But first there's something else. Something Mike in particular should note.' The detective paused to allow this to register. 'You were dead right to phone me when you did, Stella.'

She gave him an almost shy smile, but did not interrupt. She was also avoiding misdirecting a glance towards Capper, who sat wooden-faced. He was growing a sneaky feeling that somehow he had become responsible for the intrusion of violence into a set of circumstances he found more than a little baffling.

'By doing so you brought me into this business, Stella,' Bull went on with his explanation, 'and my entry may have to become official. But at this stage I'm not sure. So hear the rest of it. Beecham is alive with his skull badly creased. But by rights he should be dead and I'd most likely be the cop with a murder case to deal with. Whoever shot him was playing for keeps. No doubt about that. But because Beecham wasn't on his own the gunman was in a hurry. I can't believe the shooting was done merely to scare friend Andy. The bullet wasn't fired carelessly. It reached him. Besides, there was a lot of broken glass, so most likely a second shot was fired and the second one was on target. However, I've a request to make of both of you.'

He stopped to share another look between them and let the weight of his words register.

'What about the tape?' Capper asked.

He received a reply he certainly didn't expect.

'It's because of that tape Stella took from your pocket, Mike, that I'm making this request.' Bull was taking his time, the tactic of a man who didn't want to enter into an argument. 'I've thought about what you both told me, and I'm sure there's at least a fifty-fifty chance of her being seen from outside when she did so.'

'You mean by Laughing Boy,' Capper said, frowning.

'Laughing Boy?'

'Tom Valence's name for Andy Beecham.'

Bert Whitelaw started to snigger appreciatively but

75

cut the sound short before Bull could turn to him.

'Remember,' said Bull. 'You thought Beecham had forgotten the tape, Stella. So you took it before Mike recovered. Right?'

She nodded.

'That was as soon as Beecham left. The curtains, you both agreed, had not been drawn. I'd say the odds were heavily on the stream of light from the window attracting him and he looked inside the room and saw Stella going through your pocket.'

'Put like that,' Capper agreed, 'it sounds reasonable, though I think you're over-stressing the odds, Gary. But in that case, why the hell didn't he come back and take it from her? The bloody gun was unloaded, and, anyway, I took my time, as Stella said, coming round.'

'I think that's something that will keep for the moment. We'll return to it later, however.'

Again the Yard man's words had provided a challenge to his listeners. He waited, a close observer of the others' reactions. Stella sat tense, and he knew her brain was assessing the implications of his words like a computer.

He had time for Stella Daly. She was not only a woman whose feminine good looks were of a kind of which he wholly approved, but he knew that the brain behind her lovely eyes was both swift and accurate in its functioning. He wondered again what the hell had gone wrong between her and Mike Capper. Something had. He felt it, and also a wriggling worm of regret that did not help him to retain his objectivity towards two members of the general public whom, at certain times, he had considered himself privileged to count his friends.

He knew Mike Capper to be a first-class journalist who

was free-lancing after earning an enviable reputation as a crime reporter. Mike wasn't a womanizer or a lush, and in Gary Bull's personal book of nice people Capper's name was underscored as that of a man with an old-fashioned virtue that was seldom mentioned now. Integrity. The word sounded like a smear these days of nearly men and not-quite women with sub-human instincts.

Capper and Stella were a couple who should have made a pair of special people. Instead, they had both avoided him, as he believed, for a good while past, and now behaved like near-strangers with each other. Whatever had happened to them had hurt like salt in an open wound. They were only in his office now because Stella was a woman with enough sense to decide how important it was to put first things first. He compared her clean-lined jaw with Capper's more fleshy jowls, and decided they provided an interesting study in contrasts. A couple who could have some good-looking kids if things went right with them.

'In the meantime?' asked Capper, looking up from frowning at a new set of uncomfortable thoughts.

'I want Stella's permission to bug her car.'

Most women would have protested, exclaimed, or asked why. Stella merely looked at him. But her glance was full of silent questions.

'That's going in at the deep end,' grunted Capper.

It was a comment Bull ignored. Made because Capper felt some reaction was expected from him.

'Possibly,' the Yard man said, 'she may be in danger after the shooting. I don't know. It depends, I would think, on how our Baroness friend exploits the new situation. You see,' he hurried on when he saw a puzzled

77

exchange of glances take place between his visitors, 'I want Stella under surveillance. For security reasons.'

Both Stella and Capper made soft noises as they drew breath with surprise.

'Security?' the latter queried.

Stella rallied to ask, 'You think that necessary, Gary? It does sound a bit extreme.'

Bull picked up the buff file on the inspector's desk. 'Yes, security, and yes, it's a bit extreme,' he conceded, taking the file to his own desk and sitting down to open it. He lifted his square chin, which now looked unusually pugnacious. 'There's more, my friends. I also consider it necessary for Mike to keep his Capri Ghia garaged. I'd like you, Stella, to give him lifts when feasible, keep together when travelling, so the two of you can be watched and followed at the same time—for protection. When it's not practicable, Mike, use a taxi. We haven't got the men to spare to follow both of you separately. So your co-operation will be appreciated.'

'Good God.' Capper sounded almost as stunned as he felt. 'There must be more to this business that neither Stella nor I know about.'

'There is,' Bull said grimly, rubbing the flat of his left hand over the open file. 'It's one of the reasons Bert and I were pretty prompt in joining you both at the Postboy, and that was a phone call out of the blue, I can tell you. It's a reason, too, why you're here this morning. You could both be in danger, and in a limited sense I'm responsible simply because of what you've both confided to me. It's time I made my own reaction, shared some facts with you. All off the record. O.K.?'

Stella was the first to nod her agreement. Capper followed her lead. He was feeling she had made the running so far and was entitled to what backing he could give her. He was damned sure that, twenty-four hours earlier, she had not thought to be seated in an office having the law tell her it required her car to be bugged and that the man she hadn't married should be a passenger. He could imagine how she felt. It was how he himself was feeling.

'Good,' Bull went on more briskly after pulling down his jutting chin. 'Now just listen. That's all. Because I can only tell you so much to ensure I get co-operation, and remember, my friendly scribes, not a damned syllable is for publication, and won't be until you get the high sign from me, and that may never happen.'

'As bad as that?' Capper asked, trying to infuse a lighter note into his tone.

'Worse. This could burst at the seams and spill a real mess into Interpol's lap.' Bull refused a cigarette when Capper produced a pack. 'I keep to my pipe these days, and that not too frequently,' he said. 'You two light up. Bert's trying to kick nicotine, so don't tempt him.'

He waited until Stella and Capper were drawing on their cigarettes before dropping his first bombshell.

'We're pretty sure Andy Beecham is not the real boss of that casino consortium he heads. He's only a front man. He doesn't even own the Casino Palace here in the Smoke. He has a so-called manager, Russell Peacock, who claims to be a Canadian, but Peacock gives orders to a good many people, including Mae Hawton and Jack Hawton, an estranged husband and wife who make a show of living together solely to keep their jobs. They are down here representing a group of casino operators in other parts of the country. Now something else which connects up. The Baroness Rorthy. She is just as phoney as Beecham, a showpiece to dazzle the suckers.'

Capper sucked air noisily and looked at Stella, who said quietly, 'Maybe we're the prize suckers. I begin to get a feeling Gary is right about us not getting a story.'

'I didn't put it like that, Stella,' Bull told her reprovingly.

'I know. I only want a feature. Mike has invested time for a series he may never write because the material isn't there.'

'It may be in another form. If it is, and if I can help you, Mike, I'll tell you. But it won't be at this stage, and what you've heard and what I'm about to tell you is all still off the record.'

'Let's have the rest of it, Gary,' Capper nodded. 'Next you'll tell me she isn't a baroness.'

'I'll put it this way,' Bull grinned while his sharp eyes half closed. 'Josef Rorthy, who was thirty-five days married to Elsie Baynard—'

'Elise,' Stella amended softly.

Bert Whitelaw didn't choke off his snigger this time, and Bull didn't glare at him. The superintendent said, 'Elsie to me, Stella. If I'm lucky enough to be able to pinch her because I can make a charge stick it'll be in the name of Elsie Baynard. Rorthy wasn't a baron. He was a dubious playboy of mixed Balkan lineage who was conned into believing our Elsie had a goodly inheritance. He liked fast cars and faster women and piled himself up in what he called a Rorthy Special on the Monza track in Italy, but in rather odd circumstances. The Italian Questura could never be sure whether his racing car had been tampered with or not. But they had their suspicions about one Luigi Brattelli.

80

Neither of you have heard of him?'

He waited to see them shake their heads. His audience was beginning to look bemused and mentally groping.

'It gets even more interesting,' he assured them.

Stella rubbed out the remains of her cigarette. 'Mind if I get off this chair, Gary?' she asked. 'I'm beginning to grow restive, and it isn't a good sign.'

Bull waved a hand. 'Be my guest. Walk about the place as if you owned it—as far as the door, of course.' He turned to his assistant. 'Bert, how about rustling up some coffee? Might be a suitable time for a break unless our visitors are being choked with suspense.'

Whitelaw went out and came back with a tray of filled plastic coffee cones with truncated bottoms.

'It won't poison you and it won't steady your nerves,' he said with a straight face as he handed the cones round. 'But it's wet and makes nasty stains if you spill any.'

Bull didn't take more than a sip to show he was entering into the spirit of the thing, then ploughed right on.

'Luigi Brattelli was the pilot of a plane in which Mrs Rorthy played a part by pretending to drop with a parachute, only a stand-in did the risky bit.'

'*Drop into Nowhere*,' said Capper.

Bull's brows shot up. 'You saw it?'

'I had a Press pass,' Capper explained defensively.

'And took me with him,' Stella added, looking out of a window and speaking between sips.

'Brattelli is another curious type,' Bull went on. 'She seems to collect them. Or maybe they collect her. He was known to be friendly with Lucky Luciano before that leading light of the Mafia departed an ill-spent life. Today Luigi Brattelli is friendly with Russell Pea-

81

cock, comes frequently to this country and ostensibly runs an air-freight charter service from Italy to this country, bringing in such cargoes as tyres for Italian cars, washing machines for cut-price selling, you name it he dumps it. Interpol are uneasy about his real business of freighting around Europe. They think someone is behind him, just as we in this building think someone is behind Russ Peacock and the phoney casino consortium with Andy Beecham as a well-tailored and hair-styled figurehead.'

Capper's forgotten cigarette had gone out. He dumped the charred butt in his plastic cone and watched it float against the side. He pursed his mouth.

'You're saying, in effect, Gary, that the chain of casinos Beecham heads is a legitimate front to hide an illegal operation. That it?'

He knew that, when it came down to the nitty-gritty, Bull could split the finest hair. It was so now.

'No, I'm not saying that,' he shook his head. 'You are, Mike. Your crime reporter's nose makes loud sniffs which are recognizable.'

'He might have caught a cold, Guv,' Whitelaw said with a straight face. 'You know how it is, roaming about the countryside all hours of the night.'

'You don't catch many colds inside a modern car with an efficient heater, Bert. The sniffs I meant are the kind that aid coming to a conclusion about a bad smell.'

Capper sighed heavily. 'I suppose in some quarters this kind of backchat would be considered aggro and provocative.'

Stella reminded the males present that there was a woman who wasn't amused.

'Come off it, you male wombats,' she chided the general company. 'Don't turn this into a circus act. I like the dolls in spangles and none of you are dolls, while spangles wouldn't suit any of you.'

She glanced at Whitelaw, but the inspector was watching his chief, trying to gauge Bull's reaction. The superintendent said mildly enough, 'Maybe the lady has something in her favour. After all, we're bugging her car, not yours, Mike.'

'But not quite yet,' Stella reminded the Yard man sweetly. 'I'm still making up my female mind, which will remain very open until I've heard the rest. Don't tell me you have more surprises so early in the day.'

'Three,' Bull told her. 'At least. You want them in order?'

'Please, and briefly if possible. Otherwise I might have to ask to be allowed to make notes.'

Bull grinned at her. 'If I didn't know better I'd say someone's been twisting your tail, lady.'

'Ladies don't have tails for twisting.'

'My point.' There was a hint of lewdness in his deliberate wink and the curved grin that accompanied it. 'But to relieve the suspense, Stella, let me say this. Someone is playing a dangerous game. That someone could consider you've learned too much about the Casino Palace set-up and your interest in the Baynard woman might have to be stopped. A bullet could take care of that. Now the three surprises. One, Little Mere isn't a property Mrs Rorthy inherited from her dead but phoney baron. It doesn't even belong to the man everyone thinks she will marry, Andrew Beecham, who turned her into a glamorous croupier. The freehold is owned by'—he bowed his head over a sheet in the bulky

83

file—'a property group calling itself Mayfair Commercial Estates Ltd.' He looked up. 'They happen to be the holders of the lease on the premises where the Casino Palace sees a nightly exchange of a good deal of chips and cash.'

'So Little Mere is another front,' Capper reasoned.

Bull turned some of the coloured pages in the buff file. He said slowly, 'I'd say so.' A spatulate finger levelled the tops of the pages to his satisfaction. 'Surprise number two. Ruth Bailey's husband was released unexpectedly from Parkhurst a few weeks ago. He saved a warder from a malicious attack and there was no fuss about his release. It's possible his wife wasn't told. But we know Beecham sent a car to pick him up as soon as he crossed from the Isle of Wight to the mainland. After that there is no discernible trace of him.'

'I'm becoming impressed by how much you know, Gary,' Stella told him.

'While I continue depressed by how much I don't know.' Bull looked at her speculatively. 'But you and Mike might help to rectify that.'

'Now you know how guinea-pigs feel, Stella,' Capper said.

She looked at him and decided the sort of Mitchum pout he was wearing at that moment made him rather sexy, which she decided was a fresh discovery.

'I think we give the taxpayers value for their money, all things considered,' Bull went on, ignoring Capper's comment. 'Now surprise number three.' He opened the bottom drawer of his desk. 'Listen. I'm going to run through that tape which is supposed to record a reference to the Mafia.'

The couple seated between the desks heard him click

84

a couple of switches. These clicks were followed by a faint whirring sound. The listeners waited for voices to begin talking. Nearly half a minute dragged away. Capper was first to jump to the truth.

'Wiped clean,' he grunted. 'The deceiving bitch.'

Stella's eyes were wide. She was struggling not to jump to a false conclusion. In character, she said nothing.

'Not quite clean, Mike,' Bull said. 'Hang on. A little more patience, chummy.'

Several minutes passed with only that whirring sound coming from the open bottom drawer of Bull's desk. Suddenly there was a crackling which cleared to become a pop group bashing out an oldie of the late thirties. *September in the Rain.* The electronic backing left September deluged.

The listeners heard with some amazement the group's vocal onslaught on that pulsing back-up. Suddenly voices, instruments, and electronic sound all blurred in a fading screech of sound that ended in the familiar whirring tone.

Gary Bull switched off.

'All right, friends,' he said laconically. 'That's it. No more on the rest of the spool. An old cassette recording pop, which was not quite wiped clean. Whatever it means, one thing is certain, Mike. She lied to you, played you for a sucker, and she didn't do that without having a bloody good reason. In my book, she was trying to play you off against Andy Beecham. But I can't tell you why—yet.'

He slammed shut the drawer.

'So, Stella,' he said, lifting himself out of his chair and walking round his desk to lean against the end of

85

it. 'Do we get permission to bug your car, and can we expect the co-operation we might need to ask for at short notice?'

Stella Daly's eyes were no longer wide. They stared back at Gary Bull with a look of frank inquiry. Her slow smile was spreading through a look of strain, which wasn't easy and required concentration of thought.

'One question before I say yes, Gary. Why my car, and not, say, Mike's.'

'Fair question,' Bull conceded. 'I think like a cop, Stella. A villain might decide you and Mike easier in your car than you and Mike in his. That's loaded with prejudice, so don't point it out. I know. But I want this thing out in the open. I mean whatever motivates the real purpose for running the chain of casinos and what is concealed behind that front. It's illegal, and it's big.'

'And of course you have no idea what it is,' Stella said.

'Stella,' chided Capper.

But Bull wasn't put out. 'Oh, I've an idea. A whole sack of ideas, which I'm not prepared to empty into your lap, lady.'

Stella Daly looked warm from the beginnings of embarrassment.

'How can I say no?' she asked, with a small shrug.

'You can't,' Bull told her bluntly, almost brutally, 'and not be held with Mike for formal questioning.'

'About what, for God's sake?' Capper asked sharply. He was aware that the Yard superintendent was purposely resorting again to shock tactics.

Gary Bull sighed theatrically, then shook his head and rinsed his face in a beefy hand. He dropped his hand to his side and looked pained, as though he had to deal with dullards.

'It's at least on the cards that Beecham might die. If he did that I'd be talking to you about murder. That's when any inquiry gets rough.'

At that hour on the same morning Gary Bull wasn't the only one in London with murder and its implications looming as a threat on his mental horizon.

In his bachelor flat set behind and above the top floor of the building housing the Casino Palace, a brown-skinned man with balding hair waved tightly against both sides of his oval-shaped skull tugged his knee-length triple-blue dressing-gown of Thai silk around his lean flanks, reknotted the belt with foot-long tassel ends, and picked up the phone on the top of his private bar. One of his fingers began depressing numbers on the rectangular face, like a desk adding machine's, and he stood frowning and waiting with repressed impatience, the cigar in the corner of his rat-trap mouth forgotten.

A voice at last said in his ear, 'Luigi.'

Animation flowed over the lamp-browned face of the man in the shorty blue gown.

'Russ,' he said, giving the name plenty of sibilance. It was like a snake hissing, Luigi Barrelli reflected not for the first time. 'What do you know about someone trying to burn Andy?'

The naked Italian hitched himself more comfortably on his side and waved the woman beside him to silence as she would have given voice to petulant thoughts.

'Nothing. Is the bastard dead?'

'He might be by the time you get round here. Make it fast.'

Russell Peacock cut the phone connection and drew in a slow lungful of smoke.

CHAPTER SEVEN

The blonde with the sulky mouth and sexy eyes that masked a nature as soft as granite rolled on to her back and drew the bedclothes up to her chin. She watched Brattelli shrugging into his lightweight mohair jacket and followed the way his hands buttoned it across his white-on-white turtleneck jersey of fine weave. From the breast pocket of the jacket he took a pair of folded large-framed dark glasses, fitted them to his face, and smoothed back his glossy black hair.

She admitted he looked tough and sleek and dangerous, like a panther.

'Someone's fitted a short fuse to your tail,' she sneered, jealous and angry, and not very sure of herself way down where feelings really mattered.

The dark Italian-shaped head turned and the eyes masked by the spectacles' tinted lenses studied her. He moved to the bed, lithe and soundless, and before she could prevent him had tugged down the bedclothes, exposing her nakedness.

'Did anyone ever tell you what a lousy lay you are?' he inquired, as though asking what she fancied for breakfast.

He spat on her stomach and the saliva flowed into her navel like a shiny worm.

'You stink,' he told her. 'Take a bath and don't be shy with the goddam soap. Something else. Don't get a wise lip. Understand? I don't go for broads talking back.'

His voice had not been raised, but at sound of its accented English she shivered. The Latin vowels carried an echo of menace. He lifted his right hand.

'No,' she shouted, too late.

The folded firm fingers rammed into the soft texture of her side with driving impact. The blow sliced her breath as though it was something solid on a block. Pain laced her side. She moaned.

'Don't say no to me, *prostituta*.'

He hit her again, this time with the flat of his hand, raising a red weal on her flesh. She sucked air quickly, clenched her small white teeth, and hated him with her eyes.

He walked away from the bed, already forgetting her. He stood in front of the dressing-table, viewing himself in the mirror. He distributed a few articles collected from the top of the table among his pockets. He went out without looking at the blonde uncovered on the bed.

She lay there with breasts heaving tumultuously, waiting for the storm riding her to pass. That took nearly fifteen minutes. She rolled off the bed, grabbed up a towel from the floor where she had thrown it hours before, and went into the bathroom.

Another quarter of an hour passed. She came out of the bathroom looking angry but composed, the sulky mouth firmed into a thin red line that drew her mouth in at the corners, shortening it and giving it a mean look. From the pocket of the housecoat she had hauled over her washed body she took cigarettes and a folder of matches advertising the Casino Palace. She lit a cigarette and smoked half of it slowly, flicking ash to the carpet.

She walked about the bedroom, ignoring the reflection of herself in the dressing-table mirrors. Suddenly she pressed out the red stub of the cigarette in a glass ashtray at the edge of the dressing-table, and so abrupt and forceful were the motions of her fingers that she caused a hairbrush to fall to the floor. She left it lying there, walked around the bed, to sit on the side of it before she picked up the phone.

She dialled a number she didn't have to check. When a man's voice answered she said, 'Phil, I can't take much more of him.'

The man at the other end of the line tried to soothe her with soft words. She interrupted.

'I'm not a damned mare to be given the understanding horseman treatment,' she snapped. 'Luigi is a rotten bastard and I've had all I can take.'

There were more soft words from the earpiece, but she was adamant.

'Look, I'm getting out, Phil. The bastard's started to use his fists. Well, I'm not a bloody Napoli street-walker who's paid to put up with his temper, as well as provide sex kicks. So I'm telling you. This is where I pull out.'

'Not yet—please. Before you do anything, meet my sister. Talk to her.'

'That won't change anything.'

'It just might. She's close to Peacock. She's still working on that croupier's job for you. You've only got to be patient a little longer. Have you been through his things?'

'No. The way I feel I just want out. I don't want to touch his damned things.'

'All right. Just stay there. I'll get Elise to ring you. Listen to her.'

'What'll she do? Persuade me to stay and take more of the same punishment—perhaps worse?'

'She'll show you where your interests lie and how you can get even with the bloody wop.'

'You make it sound, Phil, like she hates him.'

'Ask her. Just ask her.'

Phil Baynard rang off. He dialled his sister's flat, and as soon as he heard her familiar voice said, 'You've got a problem, sis. Luigi has been using his hands on our blonde pigeon and she's ready to take off. She needs your special handling. She hasn't even gone through his things yet, and you can guess how she comes to be able to ring me. Luigi's been summoned by his boss. You can guess also what they'll discuss.'

'Who creased Andy.'

'If the job was done because Beecham has appeared to encourage you in talking to reporters you'd better get ready to take evading action.'

'Why?'

'You want me to spell it out?'

'If your spelling's good enough.'

The cynical laugh that threatened to bruise her eardrum made her bite back words that could have caused him to ring off. And since he had rung her presumably he had something to say. Presumably about the problem he had mentioned.

'All right, sis. Just one word. C,o,p,s. Simple enough?'

'Too much so. You're saying that doctor you got to patch up Andy and take him away decided to play safe and report the shooting.'

'It comes to that. He told the local C.I.D. it was an

accident. But an automatic report would go to the Yard and be filed.'

'So it's an accident,' she reminded him.

'Don't play dumb, sis,' he advised her sharply. 'The accident bit might be swallowed, but not in this case. When they hear Andy Beecham has a gun the Yard will want the weapon traced. So take evading action. And on the way collect that blonde pigeon Luigi is now giving a hard time. And don't delay.'

He rang off.

She put down the phone slowly, as though her mind wasn't in the same room. She lit a cigarette, and after smoking for fifteen concentrated seconds consulted a private notebook she took from a locked drawer. She rang a Fleet Street number. As soon as Mike Capper's voice sounded on the line she said, 'I must see you urgently, Mike.'

'Sounds like trouble,' Capper said, his thoughts beginning to mesh at several levels at the same time.

'It might even be worse than it sounds.'

'In that case,' he told her, 'you'd better let Stella hear it at the same time. She's a very helpful person when she wants to be. And this could be one of those times. Especially if you've got some explaining to do.'

'And what's that supposed to mean?'

'If you don't know, Elise, you've wasted the price of a phone call.'

She took time to rub out her cigarette stub before saying, 'Very well, Mike. Both of you meet me at this address at three o'clock. Try not to be late, either of you.'

She rang off, but only to dial another number. This

time the girl Luigi Brattelli had ill-used answered the ring.

'Who is it?' she demanded suspiciously.

'Me, Elise.'

'The bloody Baroness, for God's sake! Well, get knotted. I told your damned brother I'm through.'

'I know.'

'He was quick off the mark, I'll say that. Well, don't waste words. I'm not being conned any more.'

'You haven't been.'

'A hundred thousand pounds, Phil said, and you agreed.'

'I'm still agreeing.'

'So far all I've had is a lot of aggro.'

'Be patient a little longer and do what I say. Go through Luigi's things. Just be careful. Bring any letter mailed from New York to Italy. But don't waste time reading it first.'

'Any letter?'

'Any, yes.'

'And where do I meet you?'

She was given the address that had been previously told to Mike Capper.

'Is that police car still tailing us?' Stella asked.

Capper glanced in the wing mirror on his side. He waited until the dark blue car came out from behind a bus and swerved in between two other cars in order to be sure of knowing where Stella would turn on the traffic lights they were approaching.

'Old faithful's still with us,' Capper informed her.

She shook her head. 'I don't think I'm ever going to get used to this cat-and-mouse business. I still can't see why Gary Bull wanted us to use my car.'

'He thinks he made it clear.'

She made a most unladylike sound with the tip of her tongue between even white teeth.

'Are you sure it's right at the next lights?'

'Yes, and then left and left again at the roundabout. I checked.'

Nearly twenty minutes later Stella Daly turned her car into a crescent-shaped parking space before a double-fronted block of flats apparently designed to accommodate middle-income tenants in Maida Vale. By the time she had nosed the car to a low wall above which neatly arranged garden plants nodded, and had locked the doors before joining Capper where he stood staring across the road in the direction from which they had come, the dark police car had stopped by the kerb.

'Suppose we wanted them in a hurry,' Stella said. 'How would they know which flat?'

Capper shrugged.

'Don't ask questions I can't answer, Stella. I've told you before, it's bad for my ego and damned frustrating. Just let's do as Gary Bull asked. Make no attempt to contact the police car crew. If they want to contact us, that's up to them. You can be sure of one thing. They're in direct communication with the Yard's Information Room.'

'I can't say that makes me feel any better,' Stella confessed a mite glumly. 'This is turning into a creepy and uncomfortable jaunt.' She caught Capper's sleeve as he would have stepped beyond her. 'Don't hurry. Give one of the men across the road time to get on to his feet and follow us. See where we go. That would make me feel better—I think.'

But no one had left the police car by the time Stella and Capper had crossed the forecourt, pushed through the large glass doors giving on to a wide foyer, and entered the hall of the block of flats, which had two lifts. They rode up to the fifth floor in the left-hand lift, and stepped out into a carpeted corridor in time to see a blonde woman wearing a yellow suit enter the other lift, the door of which whooshed shut on her and the lift began its descent.

Flat 512 was near the end of the corridor, where the block angled to provide the flats beyond with a better scenic view. They arrived to find the door open and voices coming from inside. The voices were high-pitched, feminine. As they stepped into the flat an angry woman with flushed face and snapping eyes sparking anger all but collided with them.

'And who the hell are you?' she demanded. 'Let me pass, damn it.'

Stella threw an arched look of inquiry at her companion. Capper was standing firm.

'Take it easy,' he said. 'We're here by appointment.'

'Well, you're late. He's dead.' The speaker was another blonde. She and the woman who entered the lift a short time before could have shared the same peroxide bottle. 'Now will you let me pass?' she demanded.

Behind her appeared Elise Baynard. She was striving to appear calm, but was obviously under some strain. The effect was mirrored on a face trying not to reveal shock.

'You'd better shut the door,' she said, 'and come in here, all of you.'

'If you think—' began the blonde aggressively, but was cut short in mid-plaint.

95

'Shut up, Vera, and do as I tell you. You and I have unfinished business as I recall.'

Elise Baynard was as much in charge as a conductor with a tourist party. She swept them into a room that was airless with closed windows, and furnished non-descriptly except for a massive armchair that was made to appear even larger in contrast to the small side-table drawn up close to one side of it. The small table was filled with bottles and a used glass, the large armchair with the sprawled and ungainly body of a man in rumpled suit over a shirt smelly with drying vomit. The eyes in the fleshy, rather porcine face stared with an idiot's intensity—fixed but vacant. Capper had been a crime reporter long enough to realize that the idiot's name was Death. And realization made something inside him start to curdle. He had to take a quick and very deep breath before he could speak.

'There was a woman in yellow who went down in the lift as we came up,' he told no one in particular.

'His wife,' Elise supplied with no hesitation. 'I met Vera outside and we came up together. I rang the bell and Mae opened the door.'

'Mae?' queried Stella, collecting a small frown between thoughtful eyes.

Vera, in a chair as far from the over-filled armchair as she could crouch, with her folded fists on her knees, as though she was about to pummel them, muttered, 'Here we go,' in what sounded like a breathless whisper.

'Mae Hawton,' said Elise, still very much the courier in charge of the party. 'She doesn't live here. She and Jack split up a year and more ago. But everybody's been keeping quiet about it to avoid complications.'

'Just a minute,' said Capper. 'The Hawtons. That rings

96

some sort of a bell. Not very clearly, though.'

'They're down here to look after the interests of the Northern partners in the casino syndicate whose head-quarters is the Casino Palace here in London, where, you may remember, I happen to be a croupier.'

'On and off,' Stella nodded. She still hadn't lost her frown.

Elise Baynard might not have heard her. She was now looking closely at the dead man, close enough to make her nose wrinkle when she caught a strong reek of the vomit on his clothes.

'Think I should get a doctor?'

At that moment Capper's mind was filled with a total recall of Andy Beecham as he last remembered him. When he saw the questioner had turned her head and was addressing him he mentally snapped to attention. Who was she trying to con? She knew damned well the man was dead.

'The police I think,' he said. 'Jack Hawton, if that was his name, looks dead to me. No one could act being dead as good as that. Not even a dead actor.'

The titter came from Vera before she caught hold of herself.

'Damn you, that's not funny,' she accused.

Capper's look agreed with her, but he didn't bother to explain. The ringing of the front-door bell of the flat caught all in the room by surprise except Jack Hawton. His last surprise had overtaken him some time before and was still with him.

'I'll go,' Capper said when all three women looked at him.

The two men outside were strangers, although one could have been the driver of the dark blue police car that had been their shadow from the Fleet Street area. The woman between them was certainly the yellow-clad female who had been in a hurry to get away as they arrived.

'Mr Capper?' inquired one of them, obviously the spokesman of the pair.

'Yes,' said Capper, 'and you don't have to tell me. I can guess. Superintendent Bull is on his way.'

'He said no one's to touch anything. Especially not the glass beside the body.'

Capper stood back and the two Yard men with their companion entered. The Yard man who hadn't spoken closed the door with his left heel. When they entered the room with the filled armchair it seemed over-crowded. Possibly because it was.

'How did you know he was dead?' Capper asked the woman who presumably had recently become a widow.

'By looking at him,' she said, 'and sniffing the glass.'

That hit all of them. Stella, in all innocence as Capper was aware, made to pick up the glass and lift it to her nose.

'No, Miss Daly, just leave it, like the super said,' said the plain-clothes man who had asked Capper to verify his name. 'We shan't have to wait long. So let's just sit down and be patient, shall we?'

He sounded like a grown-up dealing with fractious kids who should know better.

Vera slid off her chair. Her small fists were still knotted.

'I want to use the loo. How about it?'

'How long will you be?' asked the spokesman, trying to remain on top of a situation not included in his C.I.D. training.

98

'Not an hour longer than I need be,' Vera said sarcastically.

Head up-tilted, she marched out of the room and down a narrow corridor. The Yard man who had done the talking sighed and began moving around restively. Capper made way for him by squeezing back by the door, so he could see down the corridor. He noticed a door was open, but it wasn't the toilet in the bathroom on the other side of that door. That was at the end of the corridor. The open door opened wider to allow Vera back into the corridor. She drew the door to but did not close it which would have caused the latch to click. She almost ran to the bathroom, vanished inside for long enough to release a flush of water without pausing, and reappeared to shut the door with noise enough to be heard in the room where a strange sort of vigil was being enforced.

Capper moved before she came back into the room. She looked flushed, and the top button of her dress was undone. As she passed him she was doing it up.

He didn't get it, but worried at this piece of mystery like a dog with an unburied bone. What had Vera done in that room? Either she had left something there or she had removed something. Thinking about that top button, he was convinced her object in disappearing into the room was to leave something she had brought into the flat.

It didn't make sense, he allowed, but nor did a stranger named Jack Hawton poisoning himself. Maybe he was murdered. That made even less sense.

Stella crossed to him.

'What the hell did she want us here for?' She nodded in the direction of Elise Baynard, who had picked up a paperback despite a disapproving glance from the cop who was making with the reluctant verbals. 'Being here is a waste of time, Mike. I have better things to do.'

'So, I believe, had Jack Hawton not so long ago.'

'Don't be ghoulish.'

Capper heard the words without reaching to their meaning. He was watching Elise and Vera exchanging morse code signals with their eyes, and remembered what the former had said about unfinished business. Elise put down the paperback she had been pretending to read and said aloud to the assembled company, 'Excuse me, please.'

She walked out under the stares of the two Yard men, dignified, in complete control of herself and the tour party she had arranged without being sure how it would turn out. One of the Yard men lifted an arm, fingers splayed out, as though he would stop her progress to the door. She didn't so much as look at him or show awareness of his acute discomfiture. As his arm dropped she passed Capper and walked into the corridor.

The woman who had been explained as Mae Hawton smoothed the skirt of her yellow dress and said softly, 'Well, I'm damned. You marry a Continental baron and you are suddenly somebody able to put the peasants in their place.'

She had a twangy voice with slightly nasal overtones, as though she had practised too long competing with an electric guitar. The voice seemed to match the bony, angular face with inexpertly applied make-up out of which it came.

Vera gave another of her not quite happy titters.

'I bet you wouldn't say that to her face, dearie,' she said much too sweetly.

Mae Hawton made a show of recognizing her presence in the room for the first time. She said snottily, 'And whose bed did you crawl out of this morning—knees first?'

'Why, you bitch. You're not getting away with that.'

Vera went leaping at the other woman, who side-stepped, leaving the silent Yard man to collect Vera as though she were a bouncing ball nearing the end of its flight.

'Now, now,' he said, ramming the shapely blonde hard against him, for which he received a look of gathering interest from under Vera's long lashes.

This piece of byplay had allowed Capper to position himself to glance again up the corridor outside in time to see Elise hesitate by the partially open door. For some reason he could not explain just then he wanted to prevent her going into the room beyond, which was presumably a bedroom. She was reaching for the drop handle of the flush door when he coughed loudly.

She glanced back over her shoulder, and for one moment he saw panic in her wide lovely eyes. Before her head turned away the panic had given place to something else.

Mistrust? He thought possibly, but wasn't sure. Anyway, she continued to the end of the corridor and the bathroom door closed after her.

'What's the interest?'

The more talkative member of the Yard car crew was beside Capper, peering. Maybe Elise had seen him swimming into focus when she looked back.

Capper said, 'She beat me to it.'

The Yard man snorted. 'A right bunch of weak bladders we've collected here. Even the corpse has wet himself, or didn't you smell?'

He gave Capper a sharp look, as though trying to make up his mind about something, and turned away to watch his colleague taking Vera to her chair, escorting her as though she was something he had found and hated to surrender.

'Women,' grumbled his partner, the word just audible to Capper.

He looked at Stella, and found her eyeing him with open speculation. He had a sudden urge to ask her why that look was on her face, but neither time nor place was right. He wondered just how unlucky it really was.

Ten minutes later Bull and Bert Whitelaw arrived. The superintendent looked as though he had secret thoughts. Capper had seen him wear the same look on previous occasions on past cases. He took no notice of Capper or Stella, but seemed very pleased to meet Vera.

'Heard from your husband lately?' he inquired, making the words sound friendly.

'He was fixed, I tell you. Somebody fixed it. You ask his brother Sid.'

'Would he know?' Bull's surprise was very mild, but he was watching Vera closely.

Whitelaw was walking round the armchair holding the corpse his chief seemed to have forgotten and was certainly ignoring. Maybe, after all, the demands of the living were more urgent than those of the dead, though Gary Bull didn't always and invariably act as though he agreed.

'He's right where he should know, isn't he?' Vera countered tartly.

'And where's that?'

'As if you didn't know.'

'Just tell me, Vera.'

'Don't Vera me. You're not a friend. I'm Mrs Crane to you and every other copper, in or out of a monkey suit.'

'Vera,' Bull said, manner still mild, but registering hurt, 'don't try to be offensive. I'm better at it than you, and I can continue longer. Now, where's your brother-in-law. After all, you did suggest I should ask Sid.'

Vera looked round the room for an ally and found none. The detective who had grabbed her and held on to her a short while before looked away, finding a piece of blank wall of great interest.

'He's running the security for the Casino Palace. Ask her if you don't believe me.'

Capper expected Vera's pointing finger to be directed at Elise. It wasn't. She was pointing at Mae Hawton.

Gary Bull looked at the woman who had been singled out.

'Any reason why I shouldn't believe her?' he asked.

'No. Jack got him taken on,' she muttered.

'Ah, Jack—yes,' nodded the Yard superintendent turning to look down on the mess in the armchair. 'Not in a position to say much, is he?'

No one spoke.

The only sound came from the corpse. It was as though it was making some eerie and supernatural effort to communicate. Its mouth sagged open as unsupported face muscles relaxed, and trapped air escaped from contracting lung cavities.

'Bert,' said Bull. 'There must be a handkerchief in his

103

pocket. Tie his jaw up. Don't let it sag into the mess under his chin. And—'

Gary Bull broke off. Something had caught his eye. He moved forward and picked up the dead man's right wrist, brought it up to about four inches from his nose.

'My, my,' he said.

Capper stood to one side to look over Mae Hawton's shoulder. He saw what had interested the detective.

There was a small bright blob of dried blood on the whiteness of the dead flesh. Such as might be made by the withdrawal of a hypodermic syringe.

A compelling question drifted into Capper's mind.

Had Gary Bull entered the flat with a suspicion of what to look for?

CHAPTER EIGHT

Twenty-four hours later the amazing facts in the murder of Jack Hawton made headlines on page one of the national dailies. Lab tests proved that the dead man had absorbed enough sodium amatyl to kill after a lapse of hours. But the mind-squeezing drug had not been responsible for his death. That had come about when enough pure heroin had been released in an artery to shock his weakened system into a complete standstill. Jack Hawton's bodily functions had gone on strike. They had walked out on him and slammed the door after them.

The inference from this was inescapable.

Either Hawton had, for his own reasons, intended to commit suicide by falling asleep and not waking up but had been beaten to the death-dealing punch; or two persons had marked him down for destruction and one of them had been in a greater hurry than the first.

When Tom Valence tried to contact Capper to get some background in depth the phone in the latter's Fleet Street office went on ringing. Capper was out. After a wasted five minutes chewing mental fingernails the *Signet* editor took a chance and rang the office of Stella Daly in the building housing *Wench*. Only to discover that she too was not around.

Which seemed odd, but had a simple explanation.

Both Mike Capper and Stella were in Gary Bull's

office at Scotland Yard and feeling the pressure the superintendent was applying.

'Pure heroin,' he told them. 'That isn't come by easily. Indeed, it could only be used by a supplier. Any suggestions?'

He waited for their answers, while Bert Whitelaw fidgeted, obviously ill at ease in an atmosphere that was becoming too heavy for comfortable breathing.

'How about someone at the Casino Palace?' Capper suggested.

'I want names,' Bull snapped back.

'This Sid person and Vera's husband. I gathered they're brothers.' Stella spoke slowly, frowning over the words. 'Then there's Vera herself. She was there with our mysterious baroness.'

'So was Mae Hawton,' Capper added.

'No other suggestions?'

They shook their heads.

'How about you, Mike?' was the next startling question asked by Gary Bull.

Capper reared, a quick show of anger twisting his features.

'If that's meant to be a joke—' he began.

'Do I look like a man making jokes?' Bull growled, cutting him short.

'God, no! But to think—'

Again Capper was cut short, this time by Bull's hand moving in a savage downward slicing motion which was unmistakable.

'All right, Bert,' said Bull, taking out an already used handkerchief and rubbing his throat. 'Get it. Let's show what we've got.'

While the superintendent was blowing his nose his

assistant went to one of the cabinets lining a wall of the room, opened a drawer and took out a plastic bag. He put it on the desk at which the visitors sat, looking perplexed and very uneasy.

The bag was fastened with a piece of coloured wire twisted above the bulging shape. He untwisted the wire and opened the mouth of the bag.

'Take a look inside,' Bull invited.

Capper and Stella peered at the fine white crystals somewhat more powdery than sugar. They lifted their eyes and stared at each other.

'I'll play guessing games,' said the woman. 'Crazy as it sounds, I'll guess heroin.'

'Crazy as it sounds,' Gary Bull said, 'you're right, lady. Can you guess where it was found?'

'At the Hawton flat?'

'Way, way out.'

'The Casino Palace,' said Capper.

For that he received an odd look, afterwards shared between the two Yard men, which didn't make him feel he had been bright.

'Now here's a funny thing,' said Bull. 'I'm not sure whether that is a warmer guess than Stella's. It might be, and I've got to bear that in mind. You'd say that's reasonable, Mike?'

Capper felt he was being baited and didn't know why or what could be the purpose behind this curious gimmick play.

'I'd say nothing about this is reasonable, Gary. You asked if I could have shot the stuff into Hawton's arm.'

'That's right, I did. If I hadn't,' Bull told him, leaning forward over the desk, 'I'd be failing in a very elementary precaution. And I don't do things like that. If I did the top brass would retire me fast.'

While Capper remained looking out of his depth and completely void of understanding Stella pushed back her chair and stood up. She sounded as though she was repressing some new excitement when she said, 'You're hinting that this bag of heroin'—she pointed a finger at the open plastic bag—'is in some way connected with Mike.'

Bull grinned. It reminded her of a wolf in a zoo who smells fresh meat and has an empty stomach.

'Right on the ball, lady,' he said in his mock-comic manner which grated, as he knew it did. He had used it often on villains with tight lips and long records. 'It was found not long ago stashed under the passenger seat of a certain two-year-old Capri Ghia.'

That was news that brought Capper on to his feet.

'My car!'

'Of course your car, Mike. What the hell did you expect, running off with La Baynard and meeting Andy Beecham? It was all contrived, and you became involved because you've been pushing for that series. A lot of stuff about an almost unoccupied house that you can't prove. A damned tape that is wiped but is supposed to talk of the Mafia. Now a dead man with dope in his body and you with a pound of the muck found in your car. If I passed this on to the Drug Squad you'd be explaining from here to Christmas—if you could.'

When Capper remained silent, mouth firmly closed, Bull added, 'You've been set up, and there's only one reason. Someone doesn't like you, Mike. If the truth is known, they hate your guts, and now you're not on your own. Stella's up to her fascinating neck too.' Bull loosened his tie and slipped out of his jacket, which he draped over the back of a chair. He wiped his moist face again. 'All this is something that you, Mike, with your Fleet Street experience as a crime reporter should have expected. You've written about enough crooks and weir-dos.'

Gary Bull sounded as though he was suffering a fool not very gladly. He eyed Capper, who remained staring at the plastic bag on the table, looking as though he was still coming to terms with a hideous reality. The superintendent shook his head. He pocketed his soiled handkerchief and spoke more rationally, as though spelling out a patent truth to a dimwit.

'Why do you really think I wanted you and Stella using her car?'

'You said—'

'Don't tell me what I know, Mike.' Severity was creeping back into the Yard man's voice. It was becoming more harsh.

Stella spoke.

'You wanted to know where we went, Gary, and at the same time you had someone watch the garage where Mike keeps his Capri Ghia. Right?'

Bull tilted his head back and looked down his nose at her.

'Right. I was expecting something. I thought a bomb. Not that muck.'

He pointed at the bag on the table.

Capper flopped down on his chair. 'A bomb, for God's sake!'

'Why not?' Bull growled. 'Everybody's using bombs today. They're the in thing with all types with a devotion to violence, boyo, or don't you read the papers you help to fill? I just didn't want you and Stella blown up. At least,' he added grimly, 'not Stella. I'm not sure I can spare her just yet. But you, Mike, you're working out to be a dead loss.'

When Capper's head jerked on his neck the Yard man added, like a man making a grudging concession, 'Well, maybe not a dead one—yet. But you're not sitting very pretty right now, mister.'

Bull pulled back the chair on which his jacket was draped. He sat down, waving to Stella Daly to do the same. When she had done so he said, 'There's something we've got to get straight. Stella just about put me in the picture at the last moment, when it could have made a difference. I'll tell you why.' He paused, felt in his jacket pocket for his pipe, but changed his mind, and his hand reappeared empty. 'You have both met Sanderson of Interpol's Paris office in the past. He's been on to us. The Interpol network is trying to find out a new route for Turkish heroin to reach North America. This has been an undercover investigation that has been three years in the pipe-line. Now Interpol's sure that the stuff is being sent from a Bosphorus port to Bari, on the east coast of Southern Italy. The Rome Questura have been co-operating. From Bari it has been dispatched to somewhere outside Rome, and it has been flown hidden in selected air freight to this country.'

'Brattelli,' said Capper crisply.

Bull nodded. 'Yes, it would seem to be his operation, and you provided some of the confirmation, Mike.'

Capper looked surprised.

'Just be patient,' Bull told him. 'First, Sanderson's sure, but has no proof, that Luigi Brattelli, who met our phoney Baroness Rorthy when she was in that film *Drop into Nowhere*, did the lady and himself a service when he made sure that Josef Rorthy piled up on the Monza circuit in North Italy and the lady became a widow. But not for any reason you might imagine, my friends.'

The Yard superintendent paused to make sure he had the full attention of his audience. He had.

'Luigi Brattelli, who was friendly with Lucky Luciano, is an American and believed to be a Mafia undercover operator. When the French connection was busted the Mafia took a long-term view because of what was happening in the Middle East and elsewhere with millions going into strange pockets. Marseilles had no future for exporting heroin, so a new and unsuspected route was opened up. It's the one Sanderson has explained. The stuff is flown here from the area around Rome after being shipped from Bari. Brattelli and his crews fly regular commercial routes, but once over the coast dump the stuff. According to Sanderson the most likely place is somewhere in the country around the estuaries of the Crouch and the Blackwater in Essex. Then it is moved fast to a secret storage place and some is distributed throughout Britain through the casino syndicate headed by the Casino Palace here in London. But by far the greater amount is taken to the Milford Haven region, where it is put aboard a tanker of the Caroco fleet. As you may or may not know, Caroco stands for Carib Oil Company, and Sanderson says it is chiefly owned by Mafia money and has offices in several American States. But its oil-carrying is strictly legitimate. As such it is not only a money-spinner but also a sound cover for more secretive activities. You follow?'

His listeners both nodded, watching him intently.

The silent Bert Whitelaw, who had been over the ground from several directions with his chief, decided it was a time when he required a cigarette. He felt for his packet and offered it to Stella and Capper. Both accepted. Gary Bull brought an ashtray from the top of a filing cabinet to the table. He folded his shirt-sleeved arms, as though willing himself not to join the others in blueing up the atmosphere in the office.

'All right,' he went on. 'So we believe Brattelli is masterminding this new heroine trail from Europe to North America via this country. Sanderson is convinced of something else. There are longer-term possibilities. When North Sea oil is flowing fairly rapidly there will be tanker shipments all over, and the Caroco fleet might be picking up charters, which will mean complications for any Customs people trying to stop the smuggling of the drug.'

'No wonder it's said to be big business,' Stella said after exhaling a cloud of cigarette smoke. 'Every dollar tax free.'

'But there is heavy investment both in Europe and North America,' Bull pointed out. 'In this country the Mafia has taken over Andy Beecham's growing liabilities. Its man is of course the alleged Canadian manager, Russ Peacock. Indeed, according to Sanderson he and Brattelli run the European end of the operation that is becoming more involved each month.'

'What's going to be done about it?' Capper asked.

'A good question,' Bull acknowledged. 'Sanderson is sure the only way to produce a real and effective result is to round up both Brattelli and Peacock at the same time, with enough on both to ensure their going to prison for a long time. There is an alternative to trying them in a British court. That is to make sure the F.B.I. come up with a strong case for extradition and trial in a

Federal court in the States. Both are American citizens. Interpol are actually working on this angle now, but it's all a close-guarded operational secret. That's why no F.B.I. man can show his face over here and why even Sanderson isn't coming from Paris. Nothing is to raise the suspicions of our very wily birds who are now in the coop at the same time. So you can both see what you've blundered into. I use the word advisedly,' he added with a wry grin.

Stella knocked an inch of ash from her cigarette when she removed it from her mouth.

'Gary,' she said. 'Another question. Perhaps not so good as Mike's, but it's even more timely, I think.'

'What is it?'

'What do Mike and I do now? Obviously we're not here because you're not going to use us. So don't try to con us. At least, I'm speaking for myself, you understand.'

'For both of us,' Capper said as he pressed out his cigarette, and found his words had earned him a smile from both Bull and the lady.

Bert Whitelaw was trying to look as though he was not amused and not being noticeably successful.

'I'll tell you. I can use you. I'd like to, but I'll level with you about it,' Bull promised, tone and manner suddenly mild, as though he was pleased at having achieved something he had set out to accomplish. 'You're my only direct lead because you have both advertised your interest in getting a story from a certain lady who was brought into the operation because she knew too much, as did the late Baron Josef Rorthy, as you might have guessed. And of course once she was in her brother had to be involved with her. They probably don't know the whole set-up, but enough to make trouble, so they could be in danger.'

'Like Andy Beecham?' Capper asked.

Bull's head nodded slowly several times.

'Very much like Andy Beecham, and don't forget something. What happened to him happened when she was with him. I'll not add to that.'

'How about Jack Hawton?' Stella asked.

'I'm guessing,' Bull told her with an air of frankness, 'but there I think someone was too clever or wires became crossed, which will probably give his widow some wakeful nights—I hope. She's been making the running with Russ Peacock.'

'And Vera?'

'Well, now, Vera's something else. Her husband was in Parkhurst with the other Jack in the pack—Bailey. We've done some checking with our Intelligence unit and it looks as though her brother-in-law Sid, who was given a job by Peacock on Hawton's say-so and recommendation as strong-arm liaison man with the provincial managers in the casino syndicate being slowly taken over by Mafia cash, might have given the word to his brother, that's Vera's husband, to start the trouble that enabled Jack Bailey to play hero and earn remission of what remained of his sentence. If so, then Beecham must have paid Sid handsomely. That's the way Intelligence wraps it up.'

A silence of several seconds was broken when Capper spoke.

'Let's get it straight,' he said. 'You're saying Andy Beecham wanted Jack Bailey out.'

'That's the word I've been given. He certainly picked him up and spirited him away, as I told you before.'

'But why?'

'Maybe Beecham has a special use for Bailey.'

'Whose wife is living at that place in Surrey with the watery name,' Stella put in. 'Little Mere.'

'Well, not exactly,' Bull smiled apologetically. 'Tell the lady the strength of it, Bert.'

Both Stella and Capper turned their attention to Whitelaw, who leaned forward to say, 'It's this way. Jack Bailey's never been married. The woman who is passed off as his wife is his elder sister, who brought him up when their parents died. The effort left her with quite a palate for spiritous liquors. In short, she's a lush, folks. Beecham wanted her somewhere where she was safe while her brother was doing his bird.'

Stella rose again. She looked exasperated.

'Isn't there one single aspect of this whole business that's straightforward and what it appears to be?'

It was mostly a rhetorical question, but Bull took it as requiring an answer.

'Almost none, I'd say,' he told her. 'But that's villains for you. If they travel in a straight line they're sure it's straight only to the nick. It doesn't make for an easy life, Miss Daly.' He smiled at her frowning face. 'But do sit down. I want you to see something I've got because Mike tipped me off. I get a crick in my neck if I've got to stare up at you all the time.'

He felt for an envelope in the inside pocket of his jacket. When he produced it Stella was again seated.

'I believe the letter originally contained in this envelope was given to our phoney baroness by Vera, who has been shacking up with Brattelli while her husband Jack Crane was earning cash by getting himself deeper in trouble inside jail for the benefit of Jack Bailey, who is out. Vera used to run around with Phil Baynard, Elise's brother, so there's a strong connection. Vera isn't fussy about whose bed she bounces into and out of, so she could have been used by the Baynards. The record shows the sister will use anyone, even a freelance journalist when it suits her,' Bull added, and saw Capper fidget when the snide comment registered.

'Now this envelope,' he went on. 'Posted in New York, addressed to Luigi Brattelli at a firm registered in Milan. So it all seems kosher. Then look at the printed address on the envelope's flap. Caroco Properties, Inc., with offices in Madison Avenue. Know something else? My guess is Vera snitched the letter from Luigi Brattelli's things because she was told to get nosey by La Baynard, to whom she probably handed the letter at Jack Hawton's, where they met and Elise intended to show it. But she was too late. The man was dead. So she said nothing about the letter. Vera, on the other hand, got icy feet and took out what her silly head thought was insurance. She held back the envelope, and then decided to ditch it in case we searched her. She left it in Hawton's bedroom, not in some obvious place, but under a runner on the dressing-table. Now I wish to God we had searched them both. Then I'd have the letter, which I want very badly. It could be a piece of real evidence.'

Capper was reading the envelope as Bull finished. He dropped it on the table and Stella picked it up, stared at the wording on both sides.

'Now we've got it,' she said. 'You want us to get the letter from Elise for you, and you figure we can do this because we're supposedly after material from her.'

'Aren't you?' Bull inquired, much too innocently. 'Correct me if I'm wrong.'

'Stop stalling, damn you, Gary,' Stella snapped, her former irritation returning. 'Am I right or wrong?'

'Both, dear lady,' Bull said with soft chiding, coming as near to smirking as he could with the face nature had bestowed on him long before his birth. 'You're right that I'd like you to visit Elise and use your charm, which is considerable, and your tact, which is no less so. But I've something else for Mike. You, boyo, can more usefully approach Russ Peacock, and ask about Elise and Andy, sticking to the fiction that they may be the twentieth-century's great lovers. How does that grab you both?'

They glowered at him.

Neither felt impelled to speak just then, possibly because he had taken their breath away.

'Perhaps,' he said, 'the power of the Press isn't what it's often cracked up to be, Bert.'

Whitelaw was staring at his hands, looking as though he had just found them.

'Then, my dear Gary,' said Stella, 'you'd better surprise yourself by starting to pray—that you're wrong, boyo.'

Bull was beginning to register deep inward hurt when Burt Whitelaw started to laugh.

'I didn't do it, for Chrissakes,' Luigi Brattelli shouted. 'How many more times do I have to tell you, Russ?'

Russ Peacock twirled the half-burned cigar across his mouth from left to right without touching it with a hand.

'That was pure heroin shot into Jack Hawton, feller.

117

That spells something. Somebody wanted him dead.'

'Including you.'

'But not that way.'

'Any way so you can get into his wife's pants now the Baroness has given you the hands-off sign.'

The dead cigar rolled back across the fleshy mouth in the tanned broad face that seldom smiled and just as seldom frowned. Brattelli, whose emotions at times chased one another across his narrow Italian face that laughed too easily, stared at the eyes in the broad face. The only indication ever to what Peacock was thinking was to be found in his eyes, and then the searcher had to be in luck.

Words formed around the cigar butt. They fell into the office of the Casino Palace manager like bits of glass, not loud, not unmusical, but very brittle and with tiny spikes that could draw blood if taken wrongly.

'I don't have to take this from you, Luigi. I don't have to take crap from anyone who's lost his nerve.'

Brattelli drew back. He suddenly looked dangerous. Not that the other man appeared to notice. When Brattelli looked around the office Peacock said, 'No need for that. This place isn't bugged. You know New York's orders.'

They stared at each other. Peacock said nothing with his eyes or mouth. Brattelli too was making no verbal comment, but his eyes signalled a silent sneer, 'Yeah, and I know you, you bastard.'

The staring duel ended when Peacock said while the cigar butt was mobile between his lips, 'Someone shot at Beecham. So he'd be no loss, but he's a front, and whoever aimed at him missed. That's damned sloppy. Either shoot and don't miss or don't shoot.'

'Well, don't look that way at me, Russ. I didn't try to burn him. I was with Jack Hawton, trying to talk him into going back North like you asked, and I didn't spike his booze.'

'Or spike him with a hypo?'

'Lay off. I had trouble enough getting him to agree to think about it. He was a lazy bum or do I have to tell you news?'

'Not that news,' Peacock said, shaking his head. He rose from his stuffed leather swing-chair and walked away from the big executive-style desk with its battery of phones and green-shaded table lamp that held nearly two feet of daylight tubing. 'You got any ideas who'd want to fix Andy and Jack, both?'

Brattelli remained seated in the smaller chair he had chosen after entering the office. His long legs, encased in mohair trousers with flared bottoms, were stretched out and crossed at the ankles.

'You mean excluding present company?' he grinned and felt he had scored when something sparked behind Peacock's level stare and then went out quickly.

'That's what I mean, Luigi. Apart from you and me, and we haven't had orders.'

But he wondered when he saw the other's mouth compress, and he reminded himself not for the first time that he didn't know what letters were sent to Milan from New York. The group who sat around the big table and had instructions go out from Madison Avenue to half a dozen countries that he knew of often played their best cards very close to their vests.

All he knew was that round the big table they were agreed to develop the operation through Carib Oil tankers, which meant that some time in the future there would be a switch from Milford Haven in Wales to somewhere in the North of England, depending on when and how the North Sea oil flowed. That wouldn't put Brattelli out of business, but it would mean his, Russ Peacock's, moving up a few places, because while he could operate Brattelli's territory if the need arose, no one—but no one—could operate what he was setting up.

Then he thought of Elise Baynard. She had been useful, heading off the noses from the media, but he was now less sure of her value. Reporters were becoming a nuisance and fending them off with the big act between her and Beecham had been a pain. Now there was trouble. It wasn't just threatening to arrive. It was there, living with them.

'Phil Baynard,' he said, pushing the moist butt farther across his mouth to make an exit for the words. 'Why the hell do we put up with him? He's no bloody use, he contributes nothing. He knows nothing, for God's sake.'

'He knows how to squeeze a trigger. He could have fixed Jack Hawton's booze. They were pretty close one time when Elise had the crowds packing into the Palace, tossing her chips so they could look through her clothes. They were buddy-buddies.'

'Phil moving closer to Mae through her husband? It's nothing new, Luigi.'

'Closer to Vera till I got in the way.'

'Dames,' growled Peacock. 'They louse up everything if you let 'em.' He paused, walked back slowly to the big desk, staring down at his shiny shoes, which wrapped his small dancer's feet as softly as velvet and were soundless in the pile of the carpet. 'Hold it. Vera could have fixed his drink, preparing the way for Phil Baynard or someone else.'

'Me, Russ? Meaning me?'

Brattelli wasn't even showing anger. He looked amused. Peacock's chunky shoulders shrugged, the movement loosening his voluminous dazzle-patterned tie.

'Meaning we got to talk to Phil without his sister being around. Know how we do that?'

'Sure. Take her away for a spell.'

Peacock eyed the younger man speculatively. 'Yeah, you maybe got something, Luigi.'

A phone on the big desk rang. He reached over his wide chair and picked up the receiver. 'Send her up,' he said, smiling as he replaced the receiver.

'Well, what do you know, feller? The lady's called in specially to see me about something that's come up. So let's say we're in luck and there's no time like the present, and the rest of the jazz.'

Brattelli frowned, watching the other open a drawer, from which he removed a blue case. He took a hypodermic needle from the blue case. The plunger was drawn back. There was a soapy-looking liquid in the cylinder.

Peacock held the syringe out for the other to take.

'I'll do the talking, you provide the action. Be careful with it.'

'It's loaded?'

Brattelli sounded as though he wanted to be sure.

'It's always loaded. Why not? There's always emergencies too. Like now.'

Brattelli rose and took the syringe. The blue case went back into the drawer, which was closed. Peacock sat down in his over-stuffed leather chair and straightened his flashy broad tie.

He was settled and smiling when a knock came on the door.

'Come in, darling,' he called.

CHAPTER NINE

'Look, Mike,' said Stella, 'I'll stop at the end of the road and walk back. You take the car and call on Peacock. Pick me up here when you leave, say in an hour's time. If I'm not here drive on to my place. O.K.?'

Capper looked at her and there was a tightening of his throat muscles.

'You know how long it's been since I was at your place?'

Stella's eyes turned from meeting his.

'I know,' she said, her voice more husky than she realized. 'I have remembered it several times since.'

'With regret?'

'Damn you, Mike, you want me to compromise myself with the truth?'

'I can stand it if you can.'

'Double damn you.' It was spoken more softly, and the clear eyes staring across the street but seeing little were squeezed at the corners so that they looked moist. 'Well, if it's O.K.,' she said too brightly, 'I'll be moving.'

She got out of the car and Mike Capper slid into the seat under the wheel.

'See you,' he called, turning his head and watching her walking briskly back down the street. That was one thing about her, among the many he appreciated when he could consider her rationally, Stella always had direction to determine her movements. Always. Even when he disapproved of where she was going.

Like now. He wasn't at all sure that he wanted her to

go calling on Elise Baynard unexpectedly in this fashion, despite Gary Bull and what the Scotland Yard superintendent wanted. He was minded to jump out of the car and follow her, but decided against acting impulsively.

After all, Gary Bull was also expecting him to perform. He stopped looking at the figure growing smaller in the rear-view mirror and turned the key in the ignition. He drove away unhurriedly, thoughtfully.

Stella continued to the building where Elise Baynard had what the estate agents called a flatlet on the top floor but one. That meant it was a one-bedroom flat with what those same estate agents referred to as the usual offices, which meant that no door in the self-contained mini-flat opened on to what a commercial firm would consider to be an office, even for the teenager who made the tea and licked the postage stamps.

She climbed to the floor under the penthouse and stepped out into a carpeted corridor which ran to both sides of the lift entrance. She came to the door whose number she had memorized and rang the bell.

There was no sound of movement on the far side of the door. She waited before ringing again. Again there was no audible movement until the latch gave a soft click and the door opened.

'Hallo,' she said to someone who was invisible and stepped uncertainly inside.

At once the door slammed shut behind her. She whirled about to find herself being glared at by a young man. But it wasn't the anger in his face that grabbed her attention with cold menace. It was the levelled gun in his right hand, which jerked, motioning her down the small compact hallway.

'Inside,' he said.

It was neither time nor place for argument and Stella, with particles of ice chilling her toes, stepped where the gun muzzle pointed. One pertinent fact registered in her brain. The young man with the gun looked familiar yet she knew with conviction that she had never seen him before. The truth registered when he came into the living-room of the small flat, motioned her to be seated, and then stood over her, but not too close. She hadn't a hope of jumping up and grabbing for the gun.

He looked familiar because his sister's face was known to her.

'You're Phil Baynard,' she said. 'You're like your sister, aren't you?'

'Only in looks, so don't be fooled.' There was no friendliness in his voice and the look of anger hadn't vanished from his face, though she was now not sure that she was the cause. 'At a guess I'd say you were this writer woman who wants Elise to tell you her life story.'

'Not a bad guess,' Stella said, smiling hopefully. 'I'm the writer woman who wants to do an article on her for the women readers of my paper. One article, very feminine in tone. The writer man you're probably confusing me with is Mike Capper. He wants a series on your sister for the *Daily Signet.*'

The young man nodded.

'All sounds the same to me. You're both pushing to get something from her.'

'Oh, now wait a minute,' Stella protested. 'Let's be fair about this. No one's pushing her. In fact, she's been doing quite a bit of pushing of her own lately.'

The gun covering her was elevated half an inch. It stopped moving when it covered her right eye. She swallowed and tried not to look at that round black menacing hole that she knew she couldn't out-stare.

'You and this Capper character,' Phil Baynard said, making the words sound like an accusation, 'how much have you found out?'

Stella knew this was not the moment to appear hesitant, so she said promptly, even as she became aware that the ice coating her toes was growing more chilsome, 'What Elise has told me, which isn't much. But then I don't need to know much.'

'Then why are you here?'

'I couldn't get her on the phone and time is running out,' she said reasonably.

His reply surprised her.

'Yeah, I know how it is. She didn't answer the phone when I rang. That's why I'm here, too. I told her last night. I said don't go and see Russ Peacock on your own? You know who he is?'

'Isn't he the manager of the Casino Palace?' Stella inquired with wide-eyed innocence.

'You're damned right he is. I rang up some time back to make sure she was doing what I said. No answer. I rang a quarter of an hour later. Still no answer. Now Elise isn't a person who goes out for a quarter of an hour. When she steps out she goes somewhere, you know?'

'I know,' Stella nodded, wondering if he was about to become incoherent. To help his return to straight communication she asked, 'Is that thing in your fist loaded?'

'This gun? Sure.'

'Well, do you mind turning it away? I'm scared it might interrupt us.'

He pin-pointed his eyes, which continued to watch

her for several seconds before he visibly relaxed.

'Sure,' he said. 'Now I've met you I want to talk and without interruptions.'

Grinning, he put the gun in his pocket. He revealed an enviable set of white teeth. Because she was who she was she wondered if he was good for a feature about his sister before something happened to spoil the market. Brothers on sisters was not usually stuff women panted to read. At least, not those who subscribed to *Wench*. So she was feeling dubious about the opportunity opening up when she said, 'Talk about what?'

'First, let me play host for my sister. Elise would wish that. What will you drink?'

He was smooth when he gave his mind to it. He might even be dangerous. At least, to an impressionable female. She refused to wonder why the hell he had a gun at all.

'I'd like a cup of coffee.'

'Sure? Nothing more stimulating?'

'Coffee will be stimulating enough. I'm a working girl.'

'And you've got a name.'

'Stella,' she told him. 'Stella Daly.'

'Well, I hope this is going to be a pleasure for both of us,' he said enigmatically, and his grin came back as he stuck out his right hand.

Feeling a little foolish at this insistence on a worn convention, she took it in her own. His grip was firm and the shake her hand received vigorous.

'Here,' he said, pushing cigarettes and a lighter at her. 'Relax while I make the coffee. I'm good at it. Even Peacock says that and he goes around saying English coffee is only made to pour into a sewer, where it probably came from. You can tell, Stella, he's a bastard, if you'll pardon my Gaelic.'

He went into the small kitchen and she heard him being busy while she sat and smoked and took stock of her surroundings. It was a comfortable living-room with hi-fi and a twenty-four-inch TV and a fold-away liquor cabinet as well as a dull green suite with comfortable springing, sundry tables to hold record cases, a silent clock, magazines and papers and some books as well as a few potted plants, two of them rather good specimens of African violets.

She rose and walked over to the small dining area set in an alcove that was no more than a niche in a wall. On the compact dining-table were unopened letters. Probably delivered that morning and Elise had had no time to open them. One was in a familiar long rectangular envelope. It was a magazine's envelope for normal correspondence, and the title was neatly printed in the right-hand corner. It was '*Wench*—the Magazine for a Woman's World'. Then she saw that it was a re-used envelope, and had certainly not been sent the day before from her office. The slit along the top above the printed title and stamp in the left corner had been re-sealed with transparent tape, which had just encroached over the stamp and the franking mark. She picked it up and peered at the date the letter had originally been posted. It was nearly two weeks before. Suddenly she knew that Elise Baynard had put something else in that envelope which had originally contained a letter Stella had sent. The absent woman had sealed the envelope with tape and left it among the day's post, openly on the table.

128

Why? The best way to conceal something by making it obvious enough not to attract attention? Poe and a good many of his imitators since his time had used the device of concealment by merging something hidden with the obvious. Now here was something that could be a letter sealed in one of her own re-used envelopes. She lifted it in her hand, and recalled the envelope she had been shown by Gary Bull. It had been about the same size and had been sent from New York to Milan.

Suddenly she was back in the flat where a dead man with stale vomit on his chest was the centre of gruesome attention. She was remembering what Mike had told her about the women in the corridor.

Vera Crane and Elise Baynard.

She was recalled to the immediate present by the pleasant smell of freshly poured coffee and turned about to see Phil Baynard standing behind her holding two cups.

'Methinks the lady has a long nose, albeit it is very becoming.'

She felt herself flushing, even as she met his mocking smile and decided he was too good-looking, like his sister. He handed her one of the cups and she dropped the envelope on to the other post. He motioned her to one of the chairs round the dining-table, and sat opposite her.

She was determined to remain unflustered. She sipped her coffee and said, 'It's good. Thank you. Now, that letter.'

'You don't have to apologize for feminine curiosity. I've lived with it for years, might even feel lost without it.'

She wasn't sure whether he was mocking or trying

to let her off the hook on which she had impaled herself.

'My curiosity got the better of me because I recognized the envelope. It is one in which I sent a letter to your sister some time ago. She has obviously used it to hold something else. Most likely another letter, by the feel of it.'

'Why not your own, put back in the envelope to keep safe for later reference?'

He swallowed a mouthful of coffee as he waited.

'No,' she said. 'In that case she wouldn't have used transparent sealing tape to close the envelope, nor have put the sealed envelope with today's post.'

His eyes narrowed as his brows came down in a frown and she saw some of his good looks vanish. He put down the remains of his coffee and picked up the envelope in which they were now both interested.

'Open it,' he invited, passing it to her.

'But your sister—'

'Isn't here,' he finished for her. 'And we're both nosey. Don't deny it.' As she hesitated, eyeing the envelope with doubtful gaze, he said, 'All right, it'll save time if I do it.'

He tore out the untaped side of the envelope and shook a typed letter on to the table. It was folded so that the company's name and address were upside down but clear for reading to someone who often read a letter's contents in a craned posture. The name was Caroco Properties, Inc., and the address was Madison Avenue, New York, N.Y. 10022.

Phil Baynard grinned. But this time there was little pleasure in him that produced the smile. Stella saw that he was suddenly wary. But not quite soon enough. He had been taken by surprise. Enough for him to ejaculate with soft sibilance and mutter, 'My bloody clever sister. She got Vera to produce. Very clever.'

Then he saw Stella's interest.

'You're interested?'

'Very.'

'Why?'

Stella could have walked away from the precipice she had almost willingly approached. She refused. She had an almost irresponsible desire to know what made the letter important to both Baynards, brother and sister, and why Vera Crane should have been involved.

She said, 'I've seen the envelope that carried that letter from New York to where Luigi Brattelli received it.'

He was so shocked by the news he accepted implications that only he was aware existed.

'So that's why you're here. You want to be included in the carve-up of the Mafia's dope.' Then he laughed, roughly, but with a touch of cynical amusement because he was capable of that kind of harsh appreciation. 'Well, don't get too greedy or you could end up dead before you've any idea it's about to happen.'

Like a tape unreeling in her mind was the memory of Gary Bull's words spoken recently in his office.

'Does the name Sanderson mean anything to you?' she shot at him, aware that she was being perilously impulsive but unable to refrain.

As a tactic, it was hugely successful. Indeed, the unexpected question was so much of a surprise that any guard placed on his tongue was instantly removed.

'Why? He's not over here, is he?' He wanted to know, and urgently, leaning forward to peer into her face.

'I don't think so,' she replied, aware that she was dissembling. 'Were you expecting him to be?'

The guard on his tongue hadn't yet been replaced.

'Hell, no. He told me he couldn't come and be sure his cover wasn't broken. He's known to Luigi. That's why—'

Too late, he tried to stop babbling. He looked at her with an expression compounded of resentment and shocked annoyance. When he stopped abruptly she said, 'You might as well tell me. I know Sanderson's been on to Superintendent Bull at the Yard.'

'About me?'

She shook her head. 'Your name wasn't mentioned.'

'Thank God.' He seemed to make an effort to overcome a readiness to shiver. 'After all, he did promise, and I believed him. Though why the hell I should I'm damned if I know. The bastard's blackmailing me, after all.'

She was staring at him, looking bemused and wondering if she would ever make sense of what he was saying. The answer to her last doubt came almost as she framed it.

He raised his voice as he said, giving the words rising emphasis, 'You might as well know he's using me to get facts for him about Luigi Brattelli and Russ Peacock. He wants evidence to pin them to the Mafia's shirt-tails. Not the Sicilian bunch. The New York gangsters who stay under cover and remain concealed behind legitimate commercial false-fronts.'

She nodded, watching the bright panic she had put in his eyes retreat to a hooded glow, as she said quietly, 'You did say blackmail?'

She thought, from the obstinacy she read in his face,

132

that he would refuse to clarify the allegation about Sanderson, but instead he seemed ready, upon reflection, to confide in her. Maybe all he required was the excuse that part of his secret was already shared.

He said, 'There was this Italian who had been working for Luigi who was found shot in Paris, in a back-street behind the Boulevard Magenta, and he had papers of mine in his pocket and the bullet had come from my gun, which had been stolen some time before in Rome. So that was Sanderson's deal. He believed I'd been set up, but knew the Sûreté Nationale wouldn't wear it. Besides, they're like every other police force. They prefer cases cleared up and dossiers stamped closed. Either I worked for him or he let the Sûreté decide what to do with me. You think that was a choice? Hell, how do I know the clever bastard didn't set it up himself just so he could use me?'

She had known Sanderson back in the old days when Mike Capper was a crime reporter. She had liked him and believed that her feeling of respect for a man with a dangerous international job had not been misplaced.

'I can't answer that question, Phil,' she said, still quietly but now more friendly. 'But I know Sanderson thinks Luigi Brattelli arranged Rorthy's death.'

'Josef wasn't a hell of a great man, but he was a good guy. I liked him. We got along all right and he made Elise happy. Maybe as happy as any man could make her. My sister isn't every man's choice.' He stopped, rubbed his chin. 'Be that as it may, Josef didn't deserve to be wiped out in a race where his heap had been fixed.'

'So, in that case,' Stella pointed out, 'Sanderson may be trying to stay in his own race long enough to make

133

sure Josef Rorthy's murderer is presented with an over-due bill.'

Phil Baynard stared at her as though reading more into her words that she hadn't expressed. Stella felt she was running out of inspiration to keep this dialogue moving in the right direction.

The ringing of the front-door bell was not unwelcome. They both rose, but she said, 'Better let me go answer it. You don't have to show yourself unless you have to.'

He bought that with a short nod of acquiescence. She walked from the living-room and opened the front door to goggle wide-eyed at Gary Bull. Bert Whitelaw was standing behind the Yard superintendent.

'We meet in the oddest places, Stella,' Bull said and squeezed inside, causing Stella to give way before him.

'How come?' she asked, while giving her mind to a decision she had to make before he reached the living-room.

Bert Whitelaw was now in the hall. He closed the front door just before Bull said, 'The crew of the sur-veillance car reported back when you and Mike split up. We didn't have to use a computer to decide where you'd gone. As you got inside, it's obvious somebody is at home. But it isn't her ladyship. I'd bet my next pay packet on that, unless she's taken to smoking cigars.'

Only then did she smell the stale reek of cigar smoke in the hall.

She turned towards the living-room, saying, 'You'd better meet her brother. He's got a surprise for you.' Gary Bull paused, wanting the information before check-ing it. 'He's working for Sanderson.'

'Well, I'll be damned,' said Bull. 'How about that,

Bert? Didn't I say there was an angle to this Sanderson was keeping to himself?'

'Maybe if he'd made it official it would have gone to the Drug Squad,' Whitelaw said. 'What would that have left us with?'

'One king-size bloody mess,' growled Bull, 'which I think we've collected anyway.'

Then he stalked into the living-room to take a hard look at Phil Baynard.

'I'm afraid Mr Peacock isn't in his office just now,' said the man who stood before Mike Capper and looked apologetic. 'Is there something I can do, Mr—er—'

'Capper. Mike Capper. I'm a journalist. I'm doing a series on the Baroness Rorthy and I should like Mr Peacock, as the manager of the Casino Palace, to supply me with some authentic background for which he can vouch. You're—'

Capper hesitated in turn.

'Sid Crane. I'm usually around when the casino's shut. There are always things to attend to, you know.'

'I know how it is.' Capper was giving the man a close inspection while trying not to do so too obviously. He was also debating whether he could get much from Crane. From what he had heard the man had plenty of his own actions to keep under wraps. 'Can you tell me when he'll be back?'

'I'm afraid I can't. You see, I didn't know he was out until I rang his office to take up some matter with him that I couldn't deal with. But he's like that.'

'How do you mean? Like what, Mr Crane?'

'In and out. All the time. Always on the move is Mr Peacock. But then that's his job. A man in his position can't stay put for long. Can I give him a message?'

He stood waiting patiently while Capper made up his mind. The caller ended by shaking his head.

'No message,' he decided. 'But you might tell him I'd like to make an appointment. Unless Mr Beecham is back.'

'Mr Beecham is away. I'm sorry.' The man who was presumably the casino stand-in when no one else in the management was available did his best to look as regretful as his words implied. But Capper received a seemingly unjustified impression that the man would be glad to see his back. 'Does Mr Peacock know where to ring you?'

'Possibly. But in any case I'll ring him. That'll save him bothering. Thank you, Mr Crane.'

'No bother. Sorry I couldn't be more helpful.'

Capper felt as though he had been forcibly ejected and couldn't explain the feeling. He returned to Stella's car, climbed in and drove to where he had left her walking back along the pavement. As he had not used up the full hour he decided to wait in case she showed. The hour had passed, and he was about to drive away, when he saw a familiar figure approaching.

'You'd better lock it,' said Bert Whitelaw. 'This might take a little longer than expected.'

'It has to,' said Capper. 'I wasn't expecting anything.' He climbed out of the car and locked it before looking round. 'I can't see the surveillance car.'

'Don't bother. They're on the job. That's why the Super and I are here.'

'Don't tell me Mrs Baynard, if she ever calls herself that, has come back because Peacock wasn't at the casino.'

136

'She hasn't. Her brother has,' said the inspector as he fell in step with Capper. 'And Miss Daly has been grilling him.'

Capper's step dragged. He caught the inspector's arm. 'Say that again, Bert,' he requested.

Whitelaw grinned one-sidedly, knowing he was being ribbed.

'Miss Daly's been grilling him.'

'So my ears are all right. You did say what I thought you did, even though it sounded cock-eyed.' Capper removed his detaining hand. 'Why? In fact, two whys? First, why was Phil Baynard there? Second, why the grilling and what about?'

They were standing on the kerb, to all appearances a couple of acquaintances discussing something urgent. Like which horse to back in the three-fifteen at Sandown Park.

'He was there because he didn't want his sister to call on Peacock.'

'He wasn't there, Bert. I've just come from a wasted trip, trying to do what the Super asked of me. I mean Peacock wasn't there,' Capper added quickly when he saw a blank look come over the other's face. 'Now, the second why, Bert.'

Whitelaw shook his head.

'Answering that is when it gets a bit complicated. You'd best let the guv'nor tell you.'

They fell in step again.

'You know something, Bert?' said Capper. 'I don't like it when you button up and get mysterious. It gives me an uneasy feeling. A very uneasy one, if you want the truth.'

Bert Whitelaw turned to look at him. There was an

unfathomable expression on the inspector's face.

'Whenever have I wanted anything else, Mike?' he asked blandly.

Which of course was nothing in the shape of an answer to satisfy Mike Capper. But then, he asked himself silently as they crossed the road to the flats where a police car was parked, when the hell is another question an answer to a previous one?

CHAPTER TEN

Elise Baynard's eyes opened with shuddering slowness and then almost closed again because of the glare from the bright light shining on her face.

'No,' she said, unable to make the word louder than a whisper. Then as a fog seemed to thin from enveloping her brain, she asked, 'Where am I?'

The bright light dimmed until she could open her eyes again without them hurting. She looked into the familiar face of Dr Rosen. The Hebraic features were bent over her so that she could make out the white line of bone under the taut skin covering the predatory nose. She saw his loose lips part and thought they're almost purple. Perhaps there's something wrong with his blood pressure. The thought was only words which she was not conscious of thinking deliberately.

Between the purple lips were white teeth that were uneven, she saw, and this time thought he doesn't smoke. Not and keep his teeth as white as that.

Then he was speaking and the words rung like echoes in her still fuzzy brain.

'You're here with me. You had a bad time. You collapsed and were brought here. Soon you will be feeling better. No, don't lift yourself up,' he said as she tried. 'You'll only bring on a headache if you strain.'

His left hand pressed down on her shoulder, restraining her, and this made her angry. She stopped pushing against his fingers and opened her eyes wider. She found herself staring into the insincere smile as though her glance was a fruit knife and she peeled away the skin of an orange. A pale but sallow orange. Unripe.

Tumblers were clicking and filling niches in her brain and she had an awareness that she was doing nothing directly to help them, as when she said, 'Where is Andy Beecham, doctor?'

'Now you mustn't worry yourself about Mr Beecham. He's mending nicely. Very nicely indeed.'

She didn't believe it, but again she didn't know why. She tried to recall what she knew about Dr Isadore Rosen, but there was a blockage among the cells she wished to use. Probably because she was trying too hard. She decided not to try at all and not to be curious. Surprisingly it took almost no effort to make her mind a blank.

'That's better,' said the white-coated Jewish doctor, withdrawing his hand. 'Now the nurse will bring you a drink. I want you to take it and try to go to sleep again. You will awake refreshed. Just don't exert yourself. Your body or your mind, Baroness.'

He was no longer in the room where the bright light had wakened her when she realized he had used her title. She tried not to wonder why that surprised her. She was still wandering through a labyrinth of clouded memory when the door opened with a squeak and a middle-aged nurse with a thin-lipped mouth and flint pebbles for eyes came in carrying a tray holding a plastic tumbler. The tumbler steamed sluggishly.

'Now drink this, Baroness,' said the nurse.

She set down the tray on a side-table and a firm plump arm dug along the nape of the patient's neck, lifting the head. The lip of the plastic tumbler was pushed between her lips and against her teeth.

'Drink. You want to get well again, don't you?'

It sounded as though the nurse was talking to someone else. A child. She was thinking about this when her teeth were forced apart and a thickish liquid flowed over her tongue. To avoid choking, she had to swallow it.

'There, that's better.'

She was on the point of rebelling and raising an arm to thrust the tumbler and its contents aside. Before she could do so the arm supporting her head changed position, fingers pinched the flesh between her ears under her hair and twisted. She opened her mouth and at the same time pushed her chin forward to ease the swift flow of pain which seemed to crawl high into the back of her scalp. That was when her mouth filled with the gooey fluid and she gulped it down. Her head again was freed and subsided against the pillow. The plastic tumbler banged against the tray. When the middle-aged nurse walked out she was singing softly.

> 'The leaves of brown came tumbling down,
>   Remember that September
>   In the rain...'

The door closed on the thin, reedy voice. It was like a valve closing in her mind. Quiet and darkness merged, became a soft nothing that was not comforting as it should have been.

How long she was unconscious she did not know. She came back to consciousness slowly, with the sound of voices. One was her own and she knew that her lips were moving and then that she was making responses.

She was answering questions.

She heard herself say, 'I don't know.'

'Did he tell you anything about a man named Sanderson, an Interpol agent in Paris?'

'No,' she said.

'Did he mention Sanderson?'

'No.'

'Nor about a dead man in Paris?'

'No.'

'A man who had been shot?'

'No.'

She heard the negatives spoken by herself as words on a tape, and then the music. Background music, coming softly, soothingly, as something she could remember. A memory inside a memory, like mental symbiosis, that quirk of nature whereby one organism lives inside another. Then she realized her eyes were closed. That she was keeping them closed although she was no longer asleep, and that moisture was seeping under her lashes. She was crying, and this puzzled her.

She heard Dr Rosen saying, 'We must be careful not to induce a traumatic condition. That could be dangerous.'

In a quiet but fierce rebuttal Russ Peacock's voice seemed to take shape, like something near and menacingly physical. He said, 'We want facts. We got to get what she knows, what she's been storing away in that goddam secretive way of hers. She's up to something. I know. Just as I know that damned brother is capable of selling us out.'

'You must not become obsessed with something that you fear,' said the Jewish doctor patiently.

She heard a sneering laugh and knew that was Luigi Brattelli. So they were both here, both making her weep tears that brought a sense of shame and also of guilt,

142

which she couldn't understand until the background music became clearer, more gently insistent and she recognized the tune.

September in the Rain.

The tune of the song the nurse who brought her the drugged drink had sung to herself. She remembered the tape, and there was a swift certitude in her mind that she had been here before, in a similar position, drugged and answering questions and with music in the background.

The wiped tape she had given to Mike Capper. It had originally come from here. Andy Beecham had acquired it in some way and that was significant because she knew he was here in this unlisted nursing home where Dr Rosen had been taking care of casualties Peacock wanted to have medical attention, to make sure his activities did not result in a charge of murder. He and Beecham had always called on Dr Rosen to take care of things when care was imperative and surgery often essential.

Then Peacock's voice was droning at her again.

'What do you know of the running of the casino syndicate?'

And her own: 'I know Andy Beecham is finished.'

'How finished?'

'He is only a figurehead.'

'Who is really running things?'

'The people behind Russ Peacock.'

'And they are?'

'I don't know.'

'But you suspect.' A pause. 'Don't you?'

'Yes,' she said, feeling her mouth was becoming dry and affecting her voice, 'I suspect.'

'Who do you suspect?'

'I can't say.'

'You can. You must.'

Then Dr Rosen, 'Be careful. This pressure and insistence could be dangerous.'

'I want answers, damn it. Truthful answers. You will
answer me, Elise. You hear? Answer. Tell me what you
suspect. Put a name to this suspicion you've got.'

She almost screamed the two words that tore out of
her mouth.

'The Mafia. I suspect the Mafia.'

The two words that had left her mouth seemed to
leave echoes floating around in her head, and she knew
her concentration was breaking. She might not be able
to keep her eyes shut. As long as she could do that, she
sensed, she was safe.

'I really must insist. Stop questioning her now.'

It was Dr Rosen again. He was worried. About her,
for her health. About himself, she knew, because they
had some hold on him. They? The Mafia. She answered
the question inside a complicated memory syndrome,
and felt an increase of the warm moisture under her
lashes.

'Hell, she's crying.' That was Luigi Brattelli.

'Because you are overtaxing her unconscious it is
pressure that finds relief in parts of her conscious.' Dr
Rosen sounded urgently anxious to impart a truth without knowing how.

'Quit the goddam mumbo-jumbo,' ordered Peacock.
'I don't trust head-shrinker talk.'

'It isn't that.'

'Well, shut up anyway, doc. Go and get that nurse.
We got to increase the dose or whatever's needed.'

'I protest.'

'All right, protest. But go get that damned nurse. Now, right now.'

The door opened and closed. Peacock's voice was thin with cruel purpose when he spoke.

'Give me that damned needle. I'll shoot her the works.'

'For Chrissake be careful, Russ,' urged Luigi Brattelli in a gruff voice that sounded like a stranger's. 'You gave Mae Hawton the stuff for Jack, and look what happened.'

'Yea, he got a hard fix with heroin. A real overkill, and that's always waste, feller. Now I want answers and I don't want Rosen's ears filled with what he don't have to know. Like what happened to his kid brother. We've only got him co-operating because he's trying to get the kid off the hook with the New York crowd. If he knows the kid got so out of line something had to be done about him, like permanent, he'd be no use to us. Like ever again. Now, let's cut the crap. The needle.'

'Hell, you could kill her.'

'So she ends up dead. Am I suppose to get sad? For a dame who can do her own crying. Look, she's bawling now. Like you said.'

'And the doc said—'

'I don't want what the doc said. I heard him. It makes no never-minds. The needle, damn it.'

Dr Rosen was not normally an eavesdropper. Had he been, he might have waited outside the door of the room he had left and heard news that would have brought his personal world tumbling in irreparable ruin. Instead he made for another room. He knew where to find the plump Mrs Borthwick, who had been a widow too long. She had been softening towards Beecham, attracted more by what she had read about the glamour boy of the gambling world than her genuine feelings.

The damned fool had been a nurse long enough to know what makes a homosexual. She should know she couldn't get anywhere with Beecham. The man was no more than a false façade. A little man in character, who was being eaten alive by human wolves, God help him.

The last word was more inclusive of himself than Andy Beecham. Possibly because his mind was running along such lines he paused when he came to the closed door of the room in which Andy Beecham was now convalescing. His attention was immediately caught by the patient's clearly audible words spoken to someone who was there with him.

'Did you look inside his pockets, as I asked you, Imogen?'

So he was using Imogen Borthwick, the foolish woman. Dr Rosen, for one of the very few times in his life, became an eavesdropper, even as he wryly reflected the old adage that eavesdroppers never hear any good for themselves.

'Oh, yes, Andy. I didn't like doing it. But since you said it was important I did, and I found this.'

There was a pause, presumably while the nurse was producing something she had purloined and had concealed in a pocket of her uniform.

'A newspaper cutting?'

'Yes. From a New York paper.'

'Where was it?'

'In the wallet inside his coat. It was hung up in his room, the one next to where Mr Peacock is staying.'

So she had to be referring to the Italian, this Luigi

Brattelli, whom Dr Rosen not only disliked, but thoroughly distrusted. He might not seem so violent as his companion, but the evil in him was something that could be sensed. It emanated from him, like an invisible ray.

But the doctor's reflections were cut off abruptly when Beecham asked sharply, 'You've read it, Imogen?'

Imogen and Andy, for God's sake! Drooling at each other, and the woman didn't realize she was being used. And in a way that could get her killed by the savages who controlled his own life.

'Oh, yes, I read it. Poor Dr Rosen.'

That emptied the listener's mind of all save a fresh curiosity that began to awaken a new fear deep down inside him.

'If he found out he'd go berserk. This report is based on a statement issued by the F.B.I. special-agent-in-charge New York City,' Beecham said.

'So I saw. I don't quite understand what it means, Andy.'

'It means it's not just ordinary police business. The local branch of the Federal Bureau of Investigation is involved. They're Government agents, not just local police.'

'Like Secret Service?'

'Not quite. There's little secret about how they work or their objectives as a Government law-enforcement body.'

'I'm afraid it's all too complicated for me, Andy. But torture—it's awful, don't you think?'

Andy Beecham didn't say what he thought. He began to summarize for himself the gist of what the reporter for the *New York Chronicle* had written.

'It says the body was found in a gutted warehouse and that the victim had been tortured, many bones broken and holes drilled into the flesh with something like a corkscrew. Imagine that.'

'It's fiendish,' gasped the plump nurse after struggling to find the word that would best convey her feelings. 'Doesn't bear thinking about, does it?'

Again a question by her was left unanswered.

Beecham went on with his summary, as though speaking aloud to fix the words he was saying more certainly in his mind. 'The victim wouldn't have been identified only his hands weren't totally destroyed in the fire, so it was possible to check his fingerprints, and it was found he had a police record. At least he had been charged with involvement in violence thought to be the work of a gang taking orders from the Mafia. He was given a suspended sentence. But it says here he tried to free himself from the clutches of the gang and probably became suspect because he knew too much, and so he was rubbed out. Those last two words are quoted. It was when a check was made on this victim that he was established as being David Rosen, who had an older brother Isadore, a doctor, who was living and had a practice in London somewhere.'

The voice stopped. So did the beating of Dr Rosen's heart for a couple of painful seconds. It was as though he was held in the grip of a cardiac seizure. A hot flow of pain shot up from the middle of his chest, like lava from an erupting volcano, blanking his mind as the heat seemed to burn out the air in his lungs.

On the point of collapse, he hauled himself together with a great and determined effort of will. He dragged air into his aching lungs, forced motion to return to his body, and grabbed the handle of the door.

He all but catapulted into the room, a wild-eyed figure of raging despair, and from the angry gash of his twisted mouth came words couched in torment.

'Let me see. Show me—show me.'

Imogen Borthwick felt herself shrinking inside the uniform she filled amply. She opened her mouth, but in time her years of training came to her rescue. She closed it and moved quickly to shut the door.

She even clicked on the catch, as though she knew instinctively the time had arrived to take precautions.

'Where the hell have you been, Mike?' Tom Valence shouted into the phone on his desk in his *Daily Signet* office. 'I've been hunting all over London for you and couldn't raise a whisper about your whereabouts. Even tried Stella. She too was off in the blue.'

'What's the panic?' Mike Capper asked. 'I told you I would be sharing Stella's car and making tactful motions around Gary Bull until my own is released. It's all taking time and I have other commitments. I explained all that, Tom.'

'Too much time, I'd say.'

'Look, Tom,' Capper snapped, growing resentful, 'I'm not doing this for love, pal. I haven't got a line in writing from you and the *Signet* isn't paying me as at this moment. So I'm still researching. Right?'

'Wrong, Mike,' said the voice at the other end of the wire. It too sounded abrupt. 'You should go out and buy a damned paper. Bring yourself up to date. There's been a shooting and God knows what else in a private nursing-home in North London. At this moment while I'm talking, according to an A.P. flash just in, the place is surrounded by police in plain clothes and also uniformed men. They're armed. The place is run by a Dr Isadore Rosen. Name mean anything to you?'

'No. Should it?'

'He had Andy Beecham there after patching him up, and there's a rumour Baroness Rorthy is also there. A new patient. Now she's someone you should be interested in. I mean, you doing all this bloody research, boyo.'

Mike Capper dragged in a lungful of the office's stale air and stared at the familiar grimed panes in the window overlooking Fleet Street.

He said, 'Maybe this will kill the series as I had planned it, Tom. How come she's a patient there?'

'I don't know. What I've gathered is that this Dr Rosen suddenly grabbed a gun and went on a private safari. A woman named Borthwick phoned the police. They picked her up running away from the place. According to her the Baroness is in danger. But that isn't all, Mike. That Mae Hawton whose husband died after being double-killed, as it were, has found another corpse. This time at the Casino Palace. You listening, chum?'

'I'm numbed and I hear words. But as yet they're not making much sense.'

'That goes for two of us, Mike. Seems the new widow Hawton went to the club and found a few cleaners and staff doing the daily chores, but no one in the offices. She went looking for the man who looks after things when the offices are empty.'

'Sid Crane. His brother's doing time in Parkhurst. He's the one who started the bother that involved a warder Jack Bailey defended and so won remission of sentence and a quick release.'

'Can't say any of that means anything. Sounds to me like you've been over-researching the wrong stuff, Mike. But Mae Hawton found him dead. This Sid Crane.' Tom Valence paused to yell at someone in the open door of his office. His voice came back on the line, sharper, somewhat more impatient. 'Someone had beaten his face in. Messy business. As you've already guessed, the Casino Palace won't be opening its doors today. The Peacock man isn't available and for a bloody good reason. He's got one of Dr Rosen's bullets in his gut, according to this Borthwick nurse person who got away. Now I don't have to lay it on the line, do I, Mike? Get the inside story so we can run it Sunday. By-line, two-page inside spread, the lot. Just keep it inside five thousand. I don't want to cut what I'm paying for.'

'What's the deadline?'

'Midnight yesterday. Hell, you know how Saturday is a pig, Mike. You won't let me down?'

'You'll get your five thousand words.'

Tom Valence rang off. Capper was still holding the receiver in a hand extended towards the instrument when the door opened. He became rigid, holding the receiver at arm's length.

In the doorway was Phil Baynard. The expression on his face was distinctly ugly because the muscles were visibly knotted with anger.

He held a levelled automatic in one hand, in the other a crumpled copy of an afternoon edition with a large black headline Capper couldn't read though he could guess the news it carried.

Baynard kicked the door shut, moved forward and tossed the paper on the desk. With the hand thus freed he took the receiver from Capper and slammed it down in its cradle. He sat on the edge of the desk and pointed the automatic's muzzle at Capper's left ear.

'You'd better read what's printed,' he said.

'I've just heard it on the phone.'

'Read, Capper.'

There wasn't much more than Valence had told Capper on the phone. It was disjointed, reports made up of phone-ins from a couple of staff man and agency flashes.

Baynard watched Capper's perusal of the printed line in heavy attentive silence.

'Now the Stop Press,' he said.

Capper turned back to the appropriate column and read: 'Nurse Borthwick believes Baroness Rorthy might be dead from overdose of sodium amatyl.'

Again Capper had trouble with his breathing.

'Now you know why you're going to help me, Capper. Refuse and I'll kill you. But first I've got something to tell you.'

He explained how Beecham and his sister had planned to move a fortune in Italian heroin, prepared from cooked Turkish opium, smuggled through Bari to plant in a warehouse outside Rome, where it was changed to morphine and then cooked to provide diacetyl morphine-hydrochloride, about 87 per cent pure, which made it lethal and expensive. A 30 per cent dose was lethal.

'I think that damned Mae Hawton sussed what was being planned, and I warned Elise to back off and forget the caper. But she'd grown greedy and wanted to show Beecham she was smarter than a bloody fairy. When a woman gets that way she can't be made to see sense. I even warned her not to see Peacock without

152

me along. But she thought she could fool him, even bring about a split between him and Luigi. I told her it was a dream. You know how I was in her place when Stella Daly showed. I had phoned a warning, I was so damned anxious what she was heading into, and she told me to stop playing little brother grown up. Her words, Capper. Then, to show me how she was on top of everything she said she had a letter sent from New York to Luigi Brattelli in Milan, which referred to new plant being opened soon in Rome and referring to a press cutting about a David Rosen. It said it was for information and appropriate action. The letter was signed by a man named Spandori. The letter had been passed to her by Vera Crane, wife of a man doing time, who had been going around with me until I let Luigi Brattelli take her off my hands. But never mind that. That was when I was half convinced by my sister she and Beecham could pull off their hijack. I still didn't let her know I was working under cover for Sanderson in Paris. You getting this clear, Capper?'

'Enough. Come to the point. That gun in your fist makes me nervous.'

Baynard's eyes had grown as bleak as grey ice and the gloom in his face might have belonged to a ruptured bridegroom.

'When I phoned that last time before she took off to talk to Peacock she told me she had earlier phoned Andy Beecham at Isadore Rosen's nursing home. She had told him about the letter produced by Vera without an envelope, and told him she was certain it meant Luigi would call on this David Rosen's brother, so he had better try and get the cutting. It might be useful.'

'This nurse the police are holding said something

about a newspaper cutting while she was hysterical,' Capper said.

'So Beecham used her, then it got leaked to this doctor who runs the place. It must have been that way. When he learned what had happened to his brother he went crazy. It's dollars to doughnuts that was the hold over him. Keeping him at long range doing as he's told so his kid brother David wouldn't be given some real lumps. Now Rosen's blown off the roof. Everything's open to the sky. When they hear of this in Saint-Cloud—'

'That's south-east of Paris. How the hell are you figuring now?'

'The new Interpol headquarters is there. As I was saying, when they hear of this there Sanderson will be hopping a plane. Before he does I want to get my own hands on the Mafia's heroin store. Then I'll see they won't pin anything on her, and I'll make sure that Paris rap against me set up by Brattelli is busted.'

'And where do I come into this?'

'I need help and you want a story. That sets us up as partners.'

'The police have my car. That leaves me with a question.'

'I have a car.'

'That isn't an answer to my question. Did you shoot Beecham and fix Jack Hawton in his flat with a heroin injection, and then leave a plastic bag of the muck in my car?'

'That's three questions. The answer to all of them is no. I don't know who shot Beecham, I believe Mae Hawton was given the sodium amatyl that spiked her old man's booze. I believe Peacock gave it to her and he had got it from Dr Rosen. That's the way the Mafia works. Wheels within wheels. All spinning fast, making movement so the outside curious eye can't see clearly. But who pushed that shot of pure heroin into him I don't know. Nor do I know who had it in for you to leave enough in your car that could suggest you were dealing in the stuff. Somebody wanted you out of the way, that's clear enough. But I can't name him.'

The dull bleak look had gone from his eyes. They were now as bright and cool as a trout's. But he fidgeted on the table edge as though it chafed like new leather on raw skin.

He went on, his gun still pointed at Capper's head:

'Nor do I know who killed Sid Crane.' In answer to a questioning look from Capper he added, 'It's on an inside page you didn't turn to. Now, any last question or piece of bloody useless advice?'

'One. I want to talk to Stella Daly.'

'Why?'

'I want to tell her to go home and stay put till she hears from me. She's another woman who is capable of taking her own line and catching up with events in her own way.'

'That's what you want to do, not why you want to do it, which is what I asked.'

Ignoring the menace of the gun only inches away, Capper jumped to his feet.

'Damn you, Baynard. I want to talk to her to make sure she's all right. I'm going to ask that sometimes infuriating woman to be my wife.'

Phil Baynard stopped looking gloomy to grin. He put his gun in his pocket.

'Now that's what I call the best reason in the world.' He gestured to the phone. 'All right. Make the call.'

Capper rang *Wench*, and was told by one of Stella's editorial assistants that she had received a phone call earlier, which had taken her to Edgware or Finchley, anyway somewhere in North London, where she had gone to pick up Baroness Rorthy, who had got away, she was told on the phone, from the nursing-home that was under siege.

Capper asked a string of questions, but the assistant had no answers to them.

He hung up and told Baynard what he had heard.

'What do you think?' he asked, point-blank.

'I think it's a damned good job I came to collect you. Miss Daly's been conned. She's gone off to collect my sister without telling anyone concerned because she was told it was urgent and because, being a journalist, she wants a story.'

'That isn't her style of journalism.'

'An exclusive is every journalist's style. You asked what I think.' Baynard slid off the edge of the old desk and stretched his back muscles. 'I think Luigi Brattelli got out of that place. He wants a hostage. So he cons your Stella into meeting him. He'll grab her for sure, and then he'll head the way we're going.'

'Where's that?' Capper asked uncertainly, for he thought he should be able to guess.

Which is what Phil Baynard also thought, for he said, 'You've already been there.'

'Hell, the penny's dropped. Little Mere, the place your brother-in-law supposedly left to your sister in his will, only he didn't. That was a pretty little piece of fiction. The place is the property of Mayfair Commercial Estates Limited.'

'That Supintendent Bull really opened up to you, didn't he.'

'To me and Stella.'

'A good reason for Brattelli picking her as a hostage, wouldn't you say?'

Capper swore.

'If he harms her.' He closed the words with an oral full-point. There was nothing left dragging after the words, merely unspoken, because for once in his life words were of no use to Mike Capper.

'If he does you'll probably have to search elsewhere for a wife, Capper. Brattelli's a bastard with women. Ask Vera Crane.'

'I've other things to do right now. I'll take your word for it, Baynard. Just let me get my own gun.'

He opened the drawer of his desk and removed the thirty-eight he had previously taken to Little Mere. He prayed silently but fervently that it wouldn't change hands so many times on the return trip. He checked that it was loaded.

The two men, united by a strange but shared objective, left the office, clattered down the stairs and crossed Fleet Street to reach the Jaguar Phil Baynard had parked in a side-street.

As the other drove off Capper asked, 'What makes Little Mere so special?'

'You don't know?'

'That's why I'm asking, damn it.'

'The people who owned it during the Second World War had a very good air-raid shelter built in the grounds. Everything laid on—electricity, water, drainage, store-room with fridge. It was like a small fort. One could live there for weeks. It was even made proof against gas attack. After the war it was useless. Too far from the house and below ground. Until Russ Peacock began looking around for a collection centre for the dope flown in by Brattelli's planes, air-dropped in South Essex, where the stuff could be collected by people in an old farm-house who provided a stopping-place for a Caroco road tanker, which shifted the stuff to Little Mere, if that's its name.'

'Why wasn't the stuff taken direct from the farm-house to where it was to be shipped? Milford Haven, isn't it?'

'That's it, in Pembrokeshire, South Wales. No, somewhere south of London was considered the ideal storage place. The farm-house had to get rid of the stuff on a short haul. Then periodically there was a longer haul to the Caroco tanker berth. That way there was no regular toing and froing from Essex to Pembrokeshire, so no suspicions were roused.'

'Not even when a Caroco road tanker pulls off the road on to the land of a private estate?'

'It isn't done like that. The road tanker calls at a garage in some place ending in 'stead'. Wait a minute—oh, I've got it. Churstead. About three miles away. The garage even has a Caroco pump and gives away trading stamps. All very obvious so it doesn't look suspicious. When a time's convenient the stuff is taken from the garage to Little Mere, and even the man in charge of the garage doesn't know what's happening under his nose.'

'God in heaven, it sounds unbelievable.'

Capper shook his head.

'Well, you'd better believe it, chummy,' Baynard said quickly, 'because if I've not got it wrong Brattelli, or whoever grabs Stella Daly, may be wheeling off into the blue and he won't want a witness to how he escaped and where he escaped to. Would he?'

It wasn't a question designed or intended to be answered, and Mike Capper remained silent, cocooned in a heavy gloom that seemed to increase as the Jag covered the miles between London and Churstead. There was not much more said between the fearful partners in a chase with an unseen quarry, but when finally they were slowing down through Churstead and Capper could see the sign 'Two Counties Garage' erected over the forecourt of a petrol station he suddenly grabbed the left arm of the man beside him.

'Look,' he hissed. 'That grey Rover parked at the side of the office.'

'What about it?'

'It's Stella's.'

CHAPTER ELEVEN

Before Stella Daly was halfway to the rendezvous she knew she had acted too impulsively. She should have phoned Mike or tried to contact Gary Bull, but the man on the phone had said, 'She's hurt and is scared of being picked up by the police. She said you would help her. Hurt and confused, very confused. But she says she'll do what you say, Miss Daly.'

It was not only pursuasive, it was genuine to Stella's surprised ears.

'I may have to advise her to go to the police,' she had told the caller.

'In that case she will do as you advise. She says she trusts you, but after what's happened to her there's no one else she can trust. No woman. As soon as I hand her over to you I shall leave.'

Going over the brief telephone conversation on the drive from Finchley towards the outskirts of Edgware, Stella became less sure that she was doing the sensible thing. Away from her office, adrift as it were, she thought of other questions she should have asked. Calls she could have made, precautionary. Once or twice she was on the point of stopping and turning about, perhaps to look for a phone booth, but she remembered that Elise Baynard was hurt, as the caller said. She had also seen the early-afternoon headlines and the brief story under them, and there was a growing curiosity inside her that urged her to perform efficiently in what was a crisis. After all, she had sought out the Baroness Rorthy and now she had the chance of coming up with something all Fleet Street would envy her obtaining.

But when she reached the corner of Southwell Avenue, as she had been instructed, it was to find the road in both directions empty. Only the occasional car was parked in front of houses built in the thirties, with small front gardens and patches of lawn beyond clipped edges lined between the road and the house with narrow flower borders. The epitome of a suburbia that was passé and didn't belong in an age of computers and high-rise dwellings, glass-walled office blocks and space rockets.

The man was crossing from one of the front gardens to her side of the car almost before she was aware of it, and the door behind her was wrenched open.

'Just drive,' he said.

'But where—' she began.

That was when he pushed the muzzle of a gun into the nape of her neck.

'No talk. Do as I say. Or else.'

She listened to the sound the words made and realized this was not someone who was bluffing. She had landed both feet in the sort of trouble of which Mike had warned her several times. 'The sort where one can end up dead,' was the way he had put it to her when she had chosen to consider the words melodramatic and incredible. Three-quarters of an hour later, the gun no longer pressed against the flesh of her neck, she realized that they were heading towards Churstead, the village three miles from Little Mere, and she understood that this was not coincidence. History was again repeating itself.

Which was anything but a comforting thought.

Because this time there was a variant.

She was no longer in contact with either Mike Capper or Gary Bull. She was on her own in a way that was utterly intimidating and chilling.

'Turn into the garage and keep your mouth shut. We're leaving your car.'

She looked without hope at the drab exterior of the 'Two Counties Garage' with the van at one end of its drive-in, with 'Caroco (U.K.) Ltd' in black on each of its yellow sides. She turned in, braked, and killed the Rover's engine. The man behind her leaned over with an outstretched gloved hand and removed the ignition key.

He got out and went to talk to someone inside a small four-square structure with the word 'Office' on a closed door, which he opened without knocking or ringing a bell. For a moment she was alone and her mind boggled at the sheer possibility of taking to her fairly sensible heels and trying to run away. From what she wasn't sure, except that she wanted no part of it.

But then her captor reappeared and she saw him for the first time, as it were, in full length, head, body, legs, and she recognized a description given in part by Gary Bull and in part by Phil Baynard when she was in the living-room of the woman whose rescue had been dangled bait to trap her.

He was Luigi Brattelli, the Italian American who was a Mafioso operating for the American crime syndicate in Europe. It was not entirely relevant, but she thought of Lucky Luciano and what she had read of the gangster chief who had been deported from the United States. This man had been friendly with the gangster who at one time operated the prostitution racket in

New York until gang-buster Dewey began a remorseless collecting of evidence that was to become a nemesis for the man who pocketed millions as the boss of a thousand pimps and the overlord of as many brothel minders and madams.

She felt sick.

'Out,' said the man with the cruel mouth and hot eyes with a glance that could sear exposed flesh. 'We're taking the van.'

This time he drove, with the door on her side locked, and his gun in the door pocket on his side. Her head began to pound with a growing migraine. She was approaching the brink of a grave calamity. There was not a thing she could do to help herself, and she now knew why. It had been knowledge she had been refusing to accept for the past hour and a half. But now denial was useless.

Her captor was going to kill her.

Some time. When he was ready. When she had become an encumbrance that was dangerous to his own survival. She sensed this as though she absorbed it through the pores of her skin. It was an awareness that was part of her being, turned by strange body chemistry into solid fact that weighed as heavy as doom in her shocked mind.

When he made the turn-off for Little Mere the house at the end of the curving drive was bathed in sunshine that gave the bricks the ruddy glare of slaked coals in a hearth's fire. The fancy was in her mind then that she was being driven to be consumed bodily by a great heat, and the fact that he turned past the sun-bathed house and along a path that led deeper into the grounds, until she could catch a glimpse of the pool from which the place took its name, in no way slaked the feeling of imminent doom that was making her head throb and to some extent impaired the sharpness of her vision.

He brought the van to a halt in a cleared space of paved ground which she saw led to steps going down to a locked door, the whole screened by surrounding trees and shrubs, which was probably why there was a swan-necked lamp over the door. A light was most likely necessary in the dark to anyone wishing to open the door.

'Out, and no tricks, mind.' He unlocked the door on her side and covered her with his slim blue-black weapon that somehow seemed to fit snugly into his berry-brown palm. 'We're going into the shelter.'

Shelter. It was the last word she would have chosen. Tomb was a word she felt more appropriate both to the look of the place and to her feelings.

She got down from the van and when he jerked the gun stepped in front of him and went down the steps. She had a grim tightness closing around her heart. This was where he had brought her to die. It was as though she was sharing a secret with herself. More than sharing. Breaking it into small pieces so that none of them could be fitted together again.

When she reached the bottom step he pushed alongside her and held her to one side while he inserted a key. The door swung inwards. He reached forward and touched a switch and light flooded a level that was another six steps down. There was moth-eaten carpet, a tiled sink, couches along a long underground wall reaching backwards and below ground level. A glance showed that there had been a time when this underground compartment had been comfortable and even inviting. But now it was in chaos. There were opened canisters from which plastic bags had been removed and cut open. There was a heavy sprinkling of white granulated powder trodden into the worn carpet, coating the furniture and fittings and crevices like snowy dust. There were torn packets, broken boxes, heaped bundles of ripped nylon from parachutes with sliced ropes, and straight ahead there was a door that was wide open, revealing the seat of a toilet. There was this white dust an inch deep on the floor, over the lid of the pan, sticking to the drop-handle cistern.

'Jesus!' exploded the man who had been brought up tottering on his narrow Italian-style footwear, while his roving eyes, appalled, took in the scene. He almost threw himself down the six inner steps, and stooped to pick up one of the opened plastic bags. He moistened a finger, dipped it into the bag and tasted carefully, like a child sampling a sherbert bag's contents.

'Cut,' he yelled. 'The bloody stuff's been cut and cut and cut.'

Stella didn't know what he meant and was mentally groping, endeavouring to recall all and everything she had read about drug peddlers cutting heroin with sugar and even French chalk, to give it bulk that would make smaller shots for addicts. Like a person in a trance, she felt her way down those inner stairs, trembling and aware that for livelong moments she was not in danger. The mind of the man she had assured herself intended to kill her was elsewhere, far from that one-time air-raid shelter that had been used as an illicit warehouse for dope smugglers.

'Who has done this—who?'

The demand began as a crazed yell of sound and

165

ended in a husky whisper, as though shock had impaired the speaker's bronchial tubes.

That was the moment there was a thin coughing sound from behind Stella, and her startled eyes saw the plastic bag ripped apart in the hands holding it. A voice behind her, somewhere up the outside concrete steps, spoke.

'The next one will smash your spine if you don't drop the shooter, Brattelli.'

She saw Luigi Brattelli open his right hand. The gun he had been gripping when she stopped in Edgware, which for most of the past two hours had been menacing her, forcing her to do what he ordered, fell to the threadbare carpet and he remained holding the ripped plastic bag while a stream of white powder sifted down over his shoes and the lower limits of his trousers. Some of the powder spilled over the gun. She watched it, fascinated, as the trigger guard began to fill and then disappeared under a small mound.

She looked round.

Standing just outside the shelter door, at the top of the inner steps, was a man she had not seen before. He was slim-waisted but with little neck and a jaw that seemed screwed down into the flesh just above his shoulders. The skin over his face was stretched tight, making the light brown eyes appear to stare.

But they were not staring at her. They were following the direction of the gun he held, which had a bulging extension that she knew instinctively for what it was.

A silencer. And silencers, Mike had told her sometime, somewhere, were only used by professionals.

'Why, man? Why do it?'

The words seemed wrung from the man holding a torn plastic bag that had emptied itself.

'You want to know?'

'Damn it, there's no sense to it. Do you know what you've done? Do you know?'

The last words were like a muted scream prompted by disbelief in what had actually happened.

'I've reduced your store of Italian-cooked heroin from a value of, say, nearly three million dollars to less than a hundred grand.'

Luigi Brattelli made a gagging noise that sounded as though it presaged an epileptic fit. He fought to overcome it, and barely succeeded.

'So you've cut it. But the rest of the stuff. It's still here, over a couple of million bucks' worth of pure H.'

'No,' said the man looking down and focusing along the bulging barrel pointed at the other. 'There's just the bags you see. The rest I flushed down that toilet. It took a hell of a time, but I managed. I nearly wore the ball-cock out.'

'You flushed away two million bucks! Just like that! D'you know the hard road that stuff travelled, all it means to the mob in New York, what was being set up, how much organization it took?'

'Maybe, maybe not. But I can imagine. But now that's all you've got to take back with you, Brattelli, and when you arrive with that cut, double cut, and triple cut horse, feller, you're not going to find your bosses happy. They won't even believe you. They only believe what they see, and they'll see someone who has lost them the best part of three million bucks of their money, and do you know what they'll do to you? Can you begin to imagine?'

There was a harsh note of quiet satisfaction in the speaker's voice, as though he was relishing the final result he had worked to obtain and thought of it gave him pleasure.

Luigi Brattelli shivered. He had read the press cutting that had been included in the envelope with the letter from Madison Avenue and signed by Toni Spandori himself, and furthermore he knew why it had been included. What had happened to David Rosen was only a part of what he could expect to be dealt to him if he was fool enough to arrive in the States and try to explain.

His one chance was to travel in the *Caroco Albatross* when she left Milford Haven and headed to Mobile, off the Gulf in Alabama. He might just get a chance to lose himself, gain time to make a contact that could intercede for him, especially now Russ Peacock was dead and the whole damned casino syndicate in Britain had been cracked wide open, with Mae Hawton back in the North squealing to her sponsors, and Vera being held as a witness by the police who wanted her to help them with their inquiries, as the limeys called it. Hell, all he had to do was not lose his nerve and find a way of getting to Milford Haven. That meant conning this damned ex-con who had him cold-decked while time was wasting.

'Tell me why you did it? Why the big hate, man? What did I ever do to you? Personal I mean.'

The man behind the gun showed his teeth in an animal-like smile.

'You and Peacock set me up in that fake publicity piece where I was filmed at the half-circle blackjack table, then playing chemin-de-fer. I was given the money to use to make it look good. But someone forgot to tell me I was using slush.'

'Slush?' Brattelli looked lost. 'What the hell's slush, for God's sake?'

'Counterfeit money, forged notes. Or have you forgotten I was arrested for being in possession of them, and I went on trial and was sent down. Shopped by you two bastards, just to get me out of the way because I'd warned Andy Beecham what was going on, how the skids were under him, and that you'd got one of the East End's Shagg gang to get my sister hooked on the hard stuff, got her joy-popping until she was no use to herself or anyone else. I even know you got that drunken bastard Jack Hawton to contact the Shaggs, Harry and Freddie, and that they were taking contracts from you and Peacock for acting as enforcers and putting on the frighteners to anyone you didn't like. Only with me it had to be different. You wanted me out of the way, permanent. But you weren't very clever. You should have removed Andy Beecham, who found out what you were up to and worked with the Baroness to fix you but good.'

The speaker was panting when he came to a halt. Stella, intrigued by a strong compulsion to understand what she was hearing, stared from one man to the other. She had heard of the Shagg family who lived in East Ham and from time to time had been mentioned in the Press when one or other of the two brothers, Harry and Freddie, appeared in court charged with some villainy, for which they were defended most ably by lawyers who doubtless were highly paid for their so-called services, which usually amounted to finding a technicality with which to defeat justice.

Mike would be able to tell her more about the Shaggs. It was a reflective, almost random thought that speared the numbness enwrapping her mind and brought back awareness of her real plight standing in the shelter between these two relentless enemies.

'You mean Beecham hid you out here?' Brattelli said in a brusque, challenging manner.

'No, he didn't know I was making trips here, to see my sister, where he'd got her hidden, hoping she'd pull out of the drug habit. Just as he didn't know he couldn't help her. It had gone too far and too fast. I tried to kill him when I thought he was in the act. That he'd helped to fix things for me to get out of the nick so he could use me without letting me know the full score.'

'You shot him.'

'I meant to kill him. But I made sure of Jack Hawton. I needn't have bothered. His bloody wife was already fixing his booze, but when you play a game this rough there's a lot of spikes you don't see first time round. I wanted him—Hawton, I mean—to get some of what he gave my sister by putting the bloody Shaggs on to her. But they'll get theirs.' He patted his breast pocket. 'I got her to tell me the lot. It's down on paper and she's signed it. And there's another statement signed by me. The cops will get the full score when and if I get un-lucky. And by God that'll be an unlucky day for a lot of double-crossing bastards.'

Luigi Brattelli knew it was of no use, but he tried because that was a moment while he was waiting, a moment he had to use to try to swing the play his way.

He said, 'You know Russ is dead, don't you? That crazy Rosen had a gun. He'd have got me too if I'd stayed. And before he died Russ went too damned far with the Baroness. Just as well the doc got him before he turned the gun on himself, because if he hadn't, then that brother of hers, he'd sure as God settle for her. That Phil Baynard is one goddamned—'

'No, Jack. Don't—don't, Jack.'

The grey-haired woman had come up unheard behind the man with the gun. Her voice was high-pitched but thin. It carried down into the shelter. Taken completely by surprise, the only armed member of that incredible tableau spun about. Almost as quick to react was Luigi Brattelli. He went down fast and grabbed up the gun he had dropped, brushed it clean of the white powder in one smooth motion, and whirled to start shooting.

The first scream seemed to blend with the first shot.

Mike Capper was twisted around in his seat, still staring unbelievingly at the disappearing shape of Stella Daly's car, drawn up on the forecourt of the 'Two Counties Garage'. It was as though he had to double-check before believing what he had seen. Although he knew convincingly that it was the car in which he had been ferried around London during the past days by Stella.

He was still gazing backward through the Jag's rear window when he heard the car's radio come on as Phil Baynard turned a switch and pressed a button.

A voice that sounded in something of a hurry finished reading out a statement by a junior member of the Government about the new row between the Health Minister and the doctors under contract to the Health Service. The junior member used a great many words in order to remain verbally in the same spot where he began the statement.

Then the hurrying voice of the newscaster tripped

over itself as he said, 'And now for the latest development in the police siege of the nursing-home in North London, where we learn there have been startling and dramatic developments, over to our reporter on the spot, Paul Bliss.'

There was some crackling and before the voice of Paul Bliss could be heard the car was swung into a left-hand lay-by and Phil Baynard braked and cut the engine.

'We'd better hear this,' he said.

He sounded like someone who had just made up his mind to walk from the dentist's waiting-room and sit down in the chair without being invited.

Then Mr Bliss's rather nasal North Country voice came intruding into the parked car, as excited as though he had ridden many leagues to bring the news to Aix.

He rattled out:

'It was a little over half an hour ago that police besieging the nursing-home forced an entry and found several persons dead, including the well-known Baroness Rorthy, who had apparently died while under sedation and receiving attention from the director of the nursing-home, Dr Isadore Rosen, who it is believed shot the man found dead in a corridor. This man is Mr Russell Peacock, also a well-known figure as the manager of the Casino Palace, London's best-known and popular gambling spot. Dr Rosen was also shot, but whether he had committed suicide is not clear at this stage. Also found in the nursing home, recovering from a scalp wound, reported to be from a gunshot, is Mr Andrew Beecham, who reputedly employed Russ Peacock. But even more mysterious is the finding by the police, alive and unharmed, of Terry Finch, a known member of the notorious Shagg gang of East London. Finch was actually being sought by the police in connection with an attack on a woman he is alleged to have been living with. There has been no further news from Nurse Borthwick, who was responsible for calling the attention of the police to the outbreak of violence in the nursing-home, but it is understood that Detective Superintendent Gary Bull of Scotland Yard is now in charge of the siege operation and is also seeking the whereabouts of Mrs Mae Hawton, who is believed to have left suddenly for an unknown destination in the North of England.'

Mr Bliss, who amazingly gave no indication of running out of breath and must have had the lungs of a rhinoceros, did at this stage pause to change key. The effect was to transform a nasal North Country squawk into a squeak echoing with the timbre of the Scottish lowlands. If he could have dropped it a full octave he might have been taken for a Geordie.

'Superintendent Bull,' he swept on, 'is anxious to interview someone who was known to be earlier at the nursing-home, but not as a patient. He is believed to have accompanied Mr Peacock. This person is Mr Luigi Brattelli, known to both Russ Peacock and Andrew Beecham. It is not known when Mr Brattelli left, but the car in which he arrived with Mr Peacock is still parked in the grounds. Someone else the superintendent is anxious to contact without delay is the brother of the dead Baroness Rorthy, Mr Philip Baynard. Attempts to reach him at an address in London have failed and an appeal is made to Mr Baynard to get in touch with the police without delay.'

There was another brief pause before Mr Bliss concluded what he had to give the listening millions.

'I have just learned,' he resumed, 'that police in the North have been alerted to report Mrs Hawton's whereabouts and the various Regional Crime Squads have been handed her description. That is all for now, except that it may be that Terry Finch is now with the superintendent being questioned. Three other persons in the nursing-home are known to be patients not involved in the shooting fracas, while no members of the staff save the director, Dr Isadore Rosen, is reported as a casualty of the violence which broke out today and the cause of which remains a mystery. However, it is believed that a statement by Chief Superintendent Bull can be expected shortly, and this may provide an answer to a riddle that is puzzling a great many persons. This is Paul Bliss, outside the nursing-home in North London where earlier today—'

There was a sharp click that had the sound of finality. Mr Bliss's unpolished vowels disappeared back into the ether whence they came.

Capper found he was holding his breath and listening to the harsh sound of his companion's breathing. He compressed his lips although tempted to speak. But he knew that any words he offered just then would be more cruel than silence.

He remained looking out of the car's window, staring at a hole in the hedgerow and the expanse of brown earth that stretched away on the far side of the hedge. He wanted to smoke, but resisted the urge to find something easy to do.

'Dead. Christ, she's dead. You heard the man. You heard, didn't you?'

Phil Baynard had found his voice and was being insistent. Capper remained looking at and through the hole in the hedge when he said, 'I heard. Your sister died in the nursing-home. That radio reporter was quite definite.'

'Yeah. Well, now it's over. We may as well turn around and go home.'

That was when Capper swung his head to face over his other shoulder. He stared at a man who was suffering and had suddenly lost his sense of direction. Possibly also his sense of proportion.

'We've come a long way,' Capper pointed out.

'So we go a long way back.'

'Without finishing what you came to do. After all, there's the business about that murder in Paris you told me about.' Capper waited for a response. None came. 'You were going to do something about that and at the same time help your sister.'

Baynard stared at him.

'What are you getting at, Capper?'

'Suppose she isn't dead.'

'The man said she was.'

'I know. But just suppose she isn't actually dead, that she isn't past recovery, and is brought back. Suppose that. Think about it for a minute. You've come a long way to help her, make sure she's not involved in something in which she became trapped at a time when death has been happening too damned frequently. Like an overkill.'

'What's that? Overkill?'

'A word implying there have been too many deaths in a situation that didn't demand wholesale slaughter.'

Baynard thought about it, shook his head. He beat a folded fist on a knee.

'I don't know. I just don't know. I can't even begin to think. My mind's a sponge. A dripping sponge that won't dry out.' He choked, ending on a soft gasping note. 'Overkill. Too much death.' He sounded as though he was savouring the words and finding them neither pleasant nor unpleasant. Merely without taste. 'It's like death is something that never throws a shadow. You understand?'

'I'm trying to,' Capper told him.

'They say coming events throw a shadow before. But not death. Or I would have been here sooner. I wouldn't have waited. Don't you understand now?'

'I think so—yes, I think I do.'

'That's a good word of yours—overkill. Let's see if we can't do something about it.'

'How do you mean?'

'Improve on it.'

Before Capper could ask him another question about his intentions he turned on the ignition and the Jag sprang into eager life. Baynard turned it out on to the road and continued in the direction he was headed when he pulled into the lay-by.

'So you're going there. To Little Mere,' Capper said.

'Correction. We're going there. We must be close to it.'

'And when we arrive?'

'We'll see, won't we?'

Capper knew the other wasn't mocking him. But neither was he sure what he was doing. He had a grave misgiving that gripped him like something physical, tearing at his body while dulling his mind. He had blundered when he had not readily agreed to Baynard turning the Jag about and returning home. At least he should have kept his damned mouth shut.

Now they were chasing into—what?

He didn't know, but was illogically convinced that they were doing the wrong thing.

He knew just how wrong when the Jag turned off into the drive that led to the familiar house set back behind its trees and shrubs that he had first seen when Baynard's sister was beside him and he was allowing himself to fall in with a plan that was to buy him a story.

They didn't hear the van until they came face to face with it. There was a blur of yellow in front of them. Baynard braked at the same instant as Luigi Brattelli. Gravel churned wildly.

Baynard stared at the other driver.

Capper stared at the passenger beside him.

It was Stella and she looked drained and scared and he knew suddenly that, no matter what broke loose in the next few instants, she wasn't going to die like Elise Baynard. He wasn't going to let it.

And he knew why.

He was going to marry her. He was not going to be a fool for the second time in his life where Stella Daly was concerned. He wrenched at the door handle next to him and almost threw himself from the Jag.

'Out!' he screamed. 'Stella, get out!'

He saw the door beside Stella swing back. The man beside her aimed a blow at her, but she was moving too swiftly and was beyond his reach as she fell out of the van and hit the ground.

'Stay down—don't move,' Capper yelled.

Then he was leaping towards where she lay, a tumbled knot of scared female with two large eyes that were looking at him in a way he had never noticed before. She was trusting him to reach her in time.

CHAPTER TWELVE

Phil Baynard leaped from the car as Brattelli fired a snap shot at the woman who had hurled herself from the van's seat beside him. The bullet dug a hole among the gravel chips where Stella had lain a split second before Capper began hauling her bodily towards the front wheels of the van.

Baynard was dragging at his gun when Brattelli fired again. It was another hurried snap shot, but this time at a larger target. The bullet smacked into Baynard's chest and dragged him upright on his toes, teetering. A man brought up short. The next bullet from Brattelli's gun drilled another hole in the chest of a man already dying on his feet. Brattelli waited until the man he had shot was collapsing before he sprang from behind the driving wheel of the van. By this time Capper had Stella propped on her unsteady feet.

'Run, Stella. Into the bushes and drop down—now, for God's sake, and let go my hand, damn it.'

He shoved her away from him, almost off her balance, but no sound came from her tight lips. She threw a single glance at the crumpled Phil Baynard and the bowed-over figure several yards away turning to shoot at her again.

Then Capper was forcing her aside and in a different direction, pitching her into an evergreen bush with dead flowers. Its shiny green leaves closed over her like an opened fan to leave her staring at a grotesque figure crouched on the ground. The man's front between his shoulders was a drying expanse of blood which left a trail on the ground as he crawled determinedly forward with a gun pushed in front of him. The muzzle was still bulging under the screwed-on silencer.

'Out of my way,' he gasped as she glimpsed the eyes full of pain.

She almost tripped over him, but then Capper was again shoving her to one side, through the bush and at a spindly tree with pale leaves.

Someone was shouting.

It could only be Brattelli, and she shrank at the foot of the thin tree, making herself into a human ball as she watched Capper, who was behaving oddly. He was staring at the crouching man with the silencer on his gun and the broad expanse of blood between his shoulders. He was shaking his head and saying, 'But Sid Crane's dead.'

She heard herself saying in a low voice, 'That isn't Crane, Mike. It's Jack Bailey, the man Beecham plotted to get out of prison.'

She saw enlightenment dawn on Capper's face as the many bright and bewildering scraps of a mystery fell into a single pattern, like the pieces of a kaleidoscope held high against the light.

Then Brattelli was coming round the bush to find them and there was a covetous look of death on his face as he raised his filled gun hand.

'All right,' he said, biting at the words as though trying to sharpen their meaning. 'So this is the way it's got to be. Suits me. I'm sure—'

But what he was sure of he had no time to explain. There was a short coughing sound that had become familiar in Stella's ears and that she knew was not produced by a human throat. Then Brattelli was staring down at the blood seeping through his clothes as it had through the clothes of Phil Baynard only seconds before.

He opened his mouth to try again.

Suddenly there was a hole in his forehead that spouted another stream of blood, and Stella screamed as she threw her arms around Mike Capper's legs.

Brattelli went down and stayed still, with his red face crushed against the ground, and the man who had killed him turned over, choked and spat blood and grinned one-sidedly, his clouding eyes seeking Capper.

'I left that package of H in your car. That was bad thinking, Mr Capper. But the way I saw it, you were a liability. You were after the story behind the front and that would have brought the cops to Ruth. She told me you were O.K., but I didn't think she could be the best judge. I was wrong. I'm sorry.'

Capper, staring at the man who had let his nerveless right hand drop the gun with the silenced muzzle, felt Stella's hands dragging at him as she levered herself first on to her knees, then to her feet. She stood beside him, but he still didn't turn to look at her. Something he saw in the blood-smeared face of Jack Bailey held his gaze as though it had been sewn to his flesh.

'Your sister—' he began.

'She's dead. Brattelli shot her, then me, but I cheated the bastard, Mr Capper. Remember that when you tell it the way it should be told. Promise me that.'

'I promise. You've just saved my life. Do you realize that? Brattelli came round that bush to kill both of us.'

'There are a couple of statements in my pocket. Take them. You see, Ruth she—'

He couldn't go on. More blood filled his mouth

180

and spilled down his front as he strove to make sound through the bubbles collecting in his flooding lungs. He made a supreme effort.

'I shouldn't have put that H in your car. It's all in what I wrote down. Superintendent Bull will know when he reads it. Once I was out I had to do what I did, make them pay for Ruth, for doing that to her. There's her statement, too, and that'll fix those other bastards, who were used by Peacock, Harry and Freddie Shagg. But you wouldn't know.'

'I know, Jack,' said Capper, 'and I'll tell the story the way you want it.'

'Thanks, Mr Capper. That's all I wanted to know. Not that I can die really happy while Russ Peacock's—'

More blood washed from his mouth. Capper felt Stella leaning against him and sobbing. He put an arm round her protectively, though what he was protecting her from he couldn't decide.

The whole bloody show was over.

Still with an arm around her, he moved closer to the man drowning in the blood he had choked up because he had over-exerted his misused body.

He stooped to be sure Jack Bailey heard his words.

'Peacock's dead. It was on the radio. A doctor named Rosen shot him. So die happy, Jack.'

Under the grim mask of blood that had spread across Jack Bailey's face his knotted features smoothed into the semblance of a smile. The light in his eyes blazed for a moment in a brightness Mike Capper was never to forget. Then suddenly it was as though a curtain had come down inside the man. The light was gone, burned out. No more blood was pumped out through the parted mouth.

Capper lifted himself.

Stella was shivering, but making no sound. Even her sobbing was now dry and soundless.

'We'd better go into the house and find a phone. I must talk to Gary Bull,' he said.

She nodded.

'Just don't leave me, Mike,' she whispered.

'I won't. After I've talked to Gary Bull we'll have to wait for an ambulance. Then Gary and Bert will probably arrive, and they'll liaise with the Surrey police, so it'll be a session. After which we'll have our own statements to make out and sign. Which reminds me, Stella. Just a moment.'

He removed her clinging hands gently and went back to Jack Bailey's body. He felt inside the jacket where again the blood it had soaked up was turning to a dark maroon-tinted mud.

He withdrew a bunch of papers, glanced at them and put them in his own pocket.

'I might as well check,' he added, and she watched him move to where Luigi Brattelli lay face down on the ground. He felt inside the dead man's jacket, but his hand came out holding nothing. She saw him patting the side pockets of the jacket.

He felt in one of them, and when he removed his hand it was holding a tightly rolled cassette. He held it up so she could see.

'It looks to me the way it all started, Stella, only this one won't be wiped clean—I hope.'

'But what is it?'

'I think it's what Elise said when she was pumped full of sodium amatyl. It should just about say enough to let Gary Bull stitch it all together.'

'Does it matter whether he does or doesn't?' she said dispiritedly.

'It'll matter to Sanderson and the Interpol crowd in Paris, and very likely to the F.B.I. in Washington and their agent-in-charge in New York, who's desperate to close in on a certain Toni Spandori, as are the members of the Rome Questura if I don't get it wrong.'

'But here in England—' She broke off and exclaimed, 'Oh! I see what you're getting at, Mike. It could all start over again, like Gary Bull hinted, this time using tankers shifting North Sea oil, unless—'

Her fresh pause was full of interrogation. Capper gave her a grim grin.

'Precisely,' he said. 'Unless all loopholes are closed now and finally. And doing that effectively will involve Interpol, Scotland Yard, the Questura, and also the F.B.I. in a far-reaching undercover operation with an international set-up able to break through a vortex of violence.'

She shook her head and suddenly laughed, but it wasn't a sound with any robust quality.

'My God, you're already stringing words like sausages and you haven't even got a typewriter in front of you. Let's get to that phone.'

She plucked dead petals of bush flowers from her clothes, turned to walk away, and stopped suddenly.

'Just a minute. I'd better get my bag.'

She went to the yellow-sided van, reached in through the open door on the passenger's side and picked up her handbag. She joined Capper and they walked back to the house together. Both became aware for the first time how the daylight was fading. It seemed curiously appropriate.

Ruth Bailey had left the front door open when she ran from the house calling to her brother. Back in the familiar lounge, Capper crossed to the phone, paused, and looking at Stella said, 'You brought Gary Bull into this business. How about if you're the one to bring him back to finish it?'

'Just make it man-to-man, Mike. I've had about all I can take.'

She dropped into the chair in which she had sat before. It seemed months ago, although the time could be measured in hours.

Capper got through to Scotland Yard and asked to speak to Superintendent Gary Bull if he was available.

'I'm afraid the superintendent's at a press conference,' he was told. 'If you would leave your name and a number we could—'

The instruction was not completed. Another voice came on the line. Gary Bull's.

'Who's calling? This is Superintendent Bull.'

'Gary. Mike Capper. I'm here at Little Mere with Stella, and there are four dead persons arranged untidily in the grounds, and two of them have made written statements which are in my pocket with a cassette which is likely to give you what you want. So make sure an ambulance is sent and then—'

Stella had crossed the room. She snatched the phone from his hand and spoke into it hurriedly.

'Gary. This is Stella. You'll have to get the Drug Squad down here to wrap up their end of the story. Oh, yes, and I shall want my car. It's parked at the "Two Counties Garage" at Churstead, where Luigi Brattelli made me drive it.'

'O.K., O.K.,' said Bull, snapping the retort testily.

'Put Mike back on for a quick word.'

When Stella passed the handset to Capper he said, 'Mike here,' and Bull went on snapping abruptly, 'How did you get there, for God's sake? You didn't go with Brattelli and Stella, I'm damned sure.'

'I didn't. Phil Baynard practically kidnapped me. Because he had been working under cover for Sanderson he was anxious to get to the underground shelter in the grounds at Little Mere, where he was sure the heroin was stored before being shifted to leave on the *Caroco Albatross*, getting ready to sail from Milford Haven to Mobile, Alabama—'

'All right, all right,' Bull shouted. 'Now you two just stay put. Don't touch anything, not even the bodies in the grounds or that shelter you mentioned. Don't make any more phone calls and don't answer any. Do nothing. O.K.? Just stay there and wait for me. If the Surrey police get there first you're waiting for me. You tell them nothing. Now you've got that clear?'

'Very clear,' Capper assured him.

Bull hung up.

He felt for his cigarettes, and when they had lit up he said, 'It could be a long wait, especially as he doesn't want us to move from here, though he didn't say what we should do about the ambulance crew. I think you'd better stay here while I see them collect the bodies. But that shouldn't take long.'

'What shall we talk about? I'll go quietly mad if we keep silent, and that isn't meant to be funny.'

'Oh, we've plenty to discuss, Stella.'

'We have?'

'We've got to fix a wedding day and decide where

we're going to live and what we'll do about furniture and our jobs and—'

'Just a moment, Mike. I haven't heard a word about why I should hold such a discussion with you.'

He saw that she was staring down at the glowing tip of her cigarette. There was more colour in her face than there had been when he dialled the Yard. In fact, she looked flushed.

'It doesn't take many words, Stella,' he said gently. 'I happen to love you and this time nothing's going to stop me marrying you. So don't get tricked by any feeling of *déjà-vu*. This is the real first time.'

He ground out his cigarette and crossed to her, picked her out of her chair, and kissed her firmly and unhurriedly and felt her quivering response. When they broke apart, he said, 'I'm still without a car till Gary Bull get's around to releasing mine. So do I get a lift?'

'I'll do better than just a lift. How about staying to breakfast?'

'Lovely, darling, only—'

The old-time quizzical kink returned to hook up her eyebrows as she echoed, 'Only?'

'Well, you remember I said Phil Baynard practically kidnapped me. That was when I'd just finished talking to Tom Valence.' He saw the arch look changing her expression and rushed on, 'He knew the series was out now Elise is dead, but a five-thousand-word centre spread for the *Sunday Signal* is on.'

'It isn't,' she said.

'Well, I was pushed, and besides I gave my word. I tried to get through to you, but you'd left the office and were going to some rendezvous out near Edgware.'

'So you got yourself driven down here. I don't see the connection.'

'I was in a hurry. First, to find you.'

'I can't quarrel with that. Is there a second?'

'Yes, I thought Valence would pay extra for the Sunday spread. I promised to do the whole story. I just about can get it into five thousand words if I keep it impersonal, but it means getting down to it later tonight, while everything's fresh in my mind.'

'Why?'

'Well, he wants to get pix to go with the copy I supply.'

'I didn't mean that, as you well know, Mike. Why were you so damned ready to be obliging? You weren't, for instance, thinking of something I did in the past which silenced any wedding bells that might have rung —figuratively speaking—and stopped our going to the Costa del Sol?'

'Quite the reverse, I was thinking of something I'd have to do in the future.'

'Like what?'

'Paying for a double cabin to Las Palmas, in the Canaries.'

She stood away from him, holding each of his biceps as though adjudging their muscular quality.

'Well, now, that's positive thinking. If you had said the Costa del Sol I think I should have hit you. I've never been there, but I hate it. Deeply and devotedly, and I shouldn't object if you said I was prejudiced. So Tom Valence is to pay for our honeymoon.'

'That about sums it up. First class all the way.'

She stroked his arms. 'When do you think you'll have those five thousand words finished, darling?'

He tried to avoid meeting her questing gaze, but found he couldn't. She had two magnets under her dark lashes, and both had full current switched on.

'Depends of course when we get away. But before breakfast.'

'It'd better be,' she smiled. 'You see, my dearest, I have no yen to lie alone in bed all of what remains of the night and the early hours of tomorrow unable to sleep because you're stringing verbal sausages on my own typewriter—which, by the way, is an old steam model, not an electric.'

'Fine,' Capper enthused tactfully. 'I can't work at speed on one of those creepy plugged-in gadgets. I'd have to stop every time it heated up, and if I'm to get finished before breakfast—'

'There's no if, Mike dear,' she told him sweetly. 'After all, like I've been telling the readers of *Wench* for some of the best years of my life, we've got to start the way we mean to go on. And you do have an office, though I don't have to remind you, I know full well.'

'There's just—'

This time he was stopped by the two-note siren—borrowed seemingly for keeps from the French *Sapeurs Pompiers*—of an approaching ambulance, whose driver was having difficulty squeezing past a Jaguar and a yellow-sided van that blocked a gravel drive on the edge of which lay two grotesque figures who were long past any aid the new arrivals could provide.

Four hours later a very tired Gary Bull saw them both to Stella's car, which Bert Whitelaw had recovered from the forecourt of the 'Two Counties Garage', just after Chief Inspector Armstrong of the Metropolitan Drug Squad was driven away in a Surrey Regional

Crime Squad's car to an airfield where a helicopter was waiting to fly him to Milford Haven.

Gary Bull pushed his head through the open window beside Capper.

'I could see you thought I ducked answering your question about Andy Beecham,' he said. 'But at the time I had my reason. I'll tell you this, Mike, now no one else is in earshot. He'll recover, and there's every chance he'll continue fronting for the casino syndicate if Mae Hawton ties a knot in her tongue, which will make some North Country operators breathe more easily. Then, when the heat's off, my guess is some City conglomerate will buy out the whole group and Beecham will be through. If he's halfway smart he'll vanish because somebody now in Parkhurst isn't going to be pleased with him when the whole damned caper is put together. Besides, the Shaggs will still be in business unless I get really lucky, and that depends on Terry Finch, the bloody little creep. O.K., Mike?'

Capper looked at him in the near-darkness.

'O.K.' he agreed. 'And thanks, Gary. I told you about the spread for Sunday. You'll get more than an honourable mention.'

Superintendent Bull removed his head from inside the car. He banged its side with the flat of his hand.

'Off with you both, and this time, Mike, finish up by making an honest woman of my favourite lady journalist.'

He turned around, started back for the house. Stella said something Capper didn't catch and let in the clutch.

Stella stirred and pushed the clothes back on her bed.

189

She opened her eyes and stared around the room. She still had it to herself, and through the curtains she had parted before undressing the sun was shining. She lay listening. She could not hear the sound of a typewriter being pounded by a man working at speed and against the clock.

She swung her long slim legs out of the bed, rose and put on her dressing-gown, and left the bedroom to walk down the corridor of the flat. She entered the room where she had left Mike Capper.

The light had been switched off, but he was still there.

She saw that his head was lowered to his chest. He had fallen asleep. She crossed to behind the chair in which he was slumped inert, as though he had been sapped. The sandwiches she had left for him had been reduced to a few crumbs and a couple of crusts. The coffee jug was empty, the ash-tray full of charred butts and sodden filter tips. There was a pile of typed pages beside the machine, the top sheet numbered 19. The sheet still in the machine was headed 'Capper: Baroness —20.' At the bottom of the page were the last three words he had typed: 'End of Copy.'

So he had finished the Sunday feature for Tom Valence. She was glad, although when she searched she could not find a reason for being so. She crossed to the window and opened it to let a draught of morning air chase away the cigarette fumes and fug. As she turned about she caught a small table with her hip. On it a pot holding a plant with cerise flowers clattered and at the sound Capper's eyes opened and quickly focused.

'Finished,' he said, 'and no vortex of violence. I forgot it and just remembered. Funny, wouldn't you say?'

'Depends, Mike. How do you feel? Wrung out?'

'I was. I'm slowly coming back to life and think I'll make it.' He gave her a slow smile. 'You got such a gentlemanly thing as a razor?'

'In the bathroom cabinet. There's a packet of blades, too. Somewhere.'

He pushed back his chair, stood, and then walked out. By the time he reached the door he was whistling. It might have been *September in the Rain*. She couldn't be sure. Probably after hearing Gary Bull play over that cassette, with Elise answering all those questions against background music turned low.

Damn, she had promised herself she wouldn't think about it. Like Gary Bull had said, it was too late for thinking and feelings and that stuff. Tomorrow had come and gone and was yesterday.

When she returned to the bedroom she heard Mike still whistling. The tune had changed, but she still couldn't be sure what it was. She sat on the side of the bed and lit a cigarette. Against advice, she found she wanted to think, but somehow she couldn't get started. Her thoughts were too muddled, and she realized she was waiting. For what was something else she didn't know. Maybe she wanted Mike to tell her he was pleased with how the five thousand words had shaped on paper, even without the vortex of violence.

She caught herself smiling. There was something she shouldn't overlook. She would be marrying a craftsman, and she couldn't have settled for less. Not with her own matching skills.

Suddenly the door opened and Mike stood there. He was freshly shaved and freshly something else. Naked, for God's sake.

'Well,' she said, 'I'm glad to see you're all in one piece.'

'I think I detect approval in that remark, but let's see if sauce for the gander is likewise sauce for the goose.' He grinned with mock lasciviousness.

She crushed out the cigarette she was no longer smoking and said, 'I thought you'd never get around to it.' She then shrugged out of her dressing-gown. 'What's brought this on?'

'Simple. I agree with Gary Bull, I ought to find a good reason for making an honest woman of you, and I've thought of the best.'

'That isn't quite how he put it.'

'So who's quibbling? I'm not. Move over, sweetheart.'

She moved crabwise obediently, looking lovely and bright-eyed with expectancy.

'On the subject of breakfast—'

Capper closed the door as she began to speak, and then interrupted, saying, 'That's a subject for which a man needs to work up an appetite. That's simple logic. But not so simple that sometimes he can get along without help and even co-operation. Like now, darling.'

He almost ran to the bed and what was waiting for him there with arms raised in welcome and certainly all the help and co-operation he could desire.